A WESTBOUND SUN

A WESTBOUND SUN

Short Stories, Memoirs and Poems

Jim Hurley

Cover painting: Esther Engelman,
Eventide, courtesy of the artist.
Author photo: Michael Coy

Print information available on the last page.

Rev. date: 06/03/2021

To order additional copies of this book, contact:
Xlibris
844-714-8691
www.Xlibris.com
Orders@Xlibris.com
825899

CONTENTS

For Jennifer, all the colors of life.

He has accrued friends who will even cheat for him a little and refuse to see his faults if they are not so glaring as to show through eyelids.

And friends are everything. For what have we wings if not to seek friends at an elevation?

—Robert Frost

Foreword

In his memoir, "A Personal Rebuke from Robert Frost," Jim Hurley recalls an astute comment from Father Raymond Roseliep, his beloved mentor and friend, who was then teaching English at Loras College. While lighting his ever-present cigar, Roseliep confided to Jim, "What I worry about is not that you won't write, but that you won't write poetry." His comment would prove prophetic.

After graduating from Loras and honorably serving in the US Navy as a journalist, Jim continued writing, yet, as Roseliep predicted, he jilted his first love—poetry—in favor of more alluring professional genres that would provide him a living. Making the most of his language skills, he launched a career helping Fortune 500 companies navigate the sometimes-turbulent waters of corporate communications. As an executive, then a consultant, he excelled for more than forty years in all areas of his field—from crisis management and public affairs to investor relations and corporate governance. Along the way he conferred privately with US presidents, dined with the British royal family, and hobnobbed with some of Hollywood's most storied celebrities, including Elizabeth Taylor, Bob Hope, Betty White, Jack Lemmon and Walter Matthau. An early marriage brought a lovely daughter, Julia Rose, whose middle name honors his mentor, Roseliep. He then met and married the love of his life, Jennifer. By any measure, Jim has led a spectacularly successful life—the kind of life anyone might praise or envy.

Yet when I first met Jim in December 2019, I sensed that in spite of all the accolades and wealth, in spite of all the profound satisfactions one might treasure from having lived a life so well, Jim recognized something was missing.

While writing his memoir on Robert Frost, Jim remembered the great books he had read in his youth, the long evenings he had spent with professors who could recite their favorite poems by heart, and the great joy he once felt when his youthful fiction and poetry won campus literary awards. Though I would not presume to read Jim's mind, I suspect that as his memories returned, with them came nostalgia, and with nostalgia came a fair measure of regret that he hadn't paid more attention to Father Roseliep's cautionary admonition. Once fully reawakened to the possibilities of a literary life, Jim, though already an octogenarian, set out on a journey to find and reacquaint himself with his first love.

I don't know what possesses a man to fall in love with poetry, nor do I know why the art can become a loyal and enduring companion in one's life. What I do know is that once poetry chooses you, you become addicted to it. Part of the attraction to poetry is that it provides us with the aesthetic experience we all crave. Unlike the anesthetic experience, which benumbs us, poetry engages all of our senses at once. It bridges the gulf between thought and feeling. It reconciles the division between mind and body. It insists upon beauty. It creates intimacies between ourselves and the snowy egret, or the tortoise, or the whale. Above all, poetry enlarges our being. It allows us to become more than ourselves, to escape our own cells of identity and to perceive the world through the eyes of others. The act of reading or writing poetry is equivalent to the mystic who finds God in a sunset or the adolescent boy who gazes upon his beloved's nakedness for the first time. In the presence of poetry, we fill ourselves with wonder and become fully alive.

Such a quickening is what I experienced as I read *A Westbound Sun* just before Christmas of last year. As I read Jim's poems, stories, and memoirs, I became immediately aware that I was in the presence of a gifted writer who introduced me to a milieu I had never before encountered. A son of the American Midwest, Jim introduced me to Iowa's rich, silted soil, to skilled horsemen who lovingly coax their animals into work, to sturdy African American firemen who stoke the boilers of the great steam locomotives that carry beef from Chicago's stockyards to markets in St. Louis, and to patient housewives who stoically endure both their husband's failings and the provincial isolation of small, family farms.

As a story writer, Jim's gift for establishing an authentic narrative voice translates into stories that are both moving and believable. In "The Broken Day of Bernie McCarville," for example, he weaves together the disparate and desperate lives of those who struggle to extract meaning and purpose from their hardscrabble conditions, then uplifts the tragedy to redeem the entire story. Similarly, "The Second Drawer Revolver" reminds me both of Richard Wright's beautiful story, "The Man Who Was Almost a Man," and William Faulkner's "The Bear," both of which focus on young protagonists who mature before our eyes as they confront the mystery and meaning of adult violence.

Though the beauty of Jim's regional color will stay with any reader forever, what truly separates this book from so many others is its display of courage. For our benefit, Jim cracks himself wide open and exposes his deepest humanity. In several poems, we overhear the confessions of a man frequently possessed of self-doubt, of a fallen idealist who struggled with the betrayal of trusted clergy members, of a despairing man caught in a battle with alcoholism so severe it nearly killed him. In sharing these autobiographical accounts, Jim connects his personal experiences to the universal truths we seek in all great literature, and he reminds us we are not alone in our many confrontations with life's obstacles.

But nowhere does this book wallow in self-pity. Though Jim presents poems that introduce us to difficulty and despair, he carefully balances those poems with others that show us how to overcome life's calamities. Like Orpheus, Jim leads us into hell but finds the wherewithal to lead us back into sunlight. These poems take us into a very human world and balance hope and despair.

This theme of indefatigable fortitude is nowhere more present than in Jim's lovely tribute to Iowa poet James Hearst, another of Jim's heroes, who, after serving in the military, broke his back in a diving accident that left him paraplegic. Undeterred by his condition and surrounded by those who loved and nurtured him back to health, Hearst worked with his younger brother as a livestock farmer and went on to publish ten books of poetry. Describing the resilience of his fellow Iowan, Jim writes,

> *You pulled the stubborn thistles from*
> *The soils and knew that more would come.*
> *When pricked by pain of back, or numb,*
> *You'd write and straighten up to plumb.*

As is so often the case, writers' tributes to others often speak as much about themselves as they do their subjects. I think this is certainly true in Jim's case. Judiciously distributed throughout *A Westbound Sun* are poems that show us again and again how a loving family, deep friendships, and perseverance conspire to defeat the darker forces in our lives. As Jim's life and book testify, he has endured to plumb his imagination and remind us that in the end the last and greatest theme is love, and for this I am most grateful.

Robert Bernard Hass
February 2021

Robert Bernard Hass is the author of Going by Contraries: Robert Frost's Conflict with Science *(University of Virginia Press, 2002), which was selected by* Choice *as an Outstanding Academic Title in 2003. He is also the author of the poetry collection,* Counting Thunder, *published by David Robert Books in 2008, and co-editor of the Letters of Robert Frost (Harvard University Press). His articles and poems have appeared in a number of journals including* Poetry, Sewanee

Review, Agni, Black Warrior Review, Literary Matters, Studies in English Literature, *the* Journal of Modern Literature, *and* The Wallace Stevens Journal. *He has won an Academy of American Poets Prize, an AWP Intro Journals Award, and a creative writing fellowship to Bread Loaf. He currently serves as Executive Director of the Robert Frost Society.*

Dear Reader

This sea of air between us curls and bends
Like warmth from nearby shoreline camps.
Within its whiffs a hand extends
To light imagination lamps.

I hope you'll hold a horse's reins with me;
Be moved by poems and poets I have met;
Descend into a story undersea;
And maybe, trace the circle routes I've flown.

These rhythms, taken from the dust
Of stars like Roseliep, Hearst and Frost
Are offered in the grateful trust
No reverence for them is lost.

At eighty-four, I rise to stand
Up straight the way my father said,
To look you in the eye, a hand
Outstretched to set forth words ahead.

I cast them, shoulder-high and one
By one behind me, to tomorrow's breeze;
Toward you, such gracious nominees,
Inside this shadow of a westbound sun.

I

Short Stories

If it is all beautiful you can't believe in it. Things aren't that way.

—Ernest Hemingway

The Broken Day of
Bernie McCarville

(Based on true events)

Sunday, August 1, 1915
Chicago, Illinois
6:20 PM

Nathan Tyrone Williams, thirty-six years old, slumps in exhaustion against a shellfish-processing plant on Wacker Drive at the edge of the Chicago River between Clark and LaSalle Streets. Painted on the brick wall above him in faded white, a sign advertises, "Fresh Oysters—Clams." Scores of people pass back and forth, their heads uniformly cast down like soldiers worn-out from a march. Rain is falling.

Before him, a mere nineteen feet from the waterfront, lies the capsized hull of the SS *Eastland*, the 265-foot excursion steamer known as "The Greyhound of the Great Lakes." Last Sunday, the *Eastland* boarded 2,500 eager vacationers and crew for a daylong cruise, that was to end in a gala evening dinner-dance. Instead, the *Eastland* never left its berth or even freed its mooring lines. Overloaded and losing its balance, the ship listed heavily to starboard and turned on its side, pivoting in slow motion from air to water in a morbid about-face.

For the past three days, Nathan Williams, the son of Mississippi indentured slaves, has been in the phalanx of hundreds of volunteers laboring with fire, police, and medical professionals in a weeklong rescue-and-recovery marathon. "They are of all social classes," the *Chicago Tribune* reports.

Eight hundred and forty-four bodies of men, women, and children have been lifted from the stricken vessel and the opaque, clammy waters of the Chicago River. They are covered with new and donated sheets and carried to the nearby Second Regiment Armory, pressed into service as a temporary morgue. Twenty-two entire families will be among them. One of the nameless dead Nathan has helped bear away to the malodorous armory will be identified as Mrs. Paul Jahnke, of New Hampton, Iowa. Her husband's limp body already lies there.

A man in the rain-drenched uniform of a Chicago fireman lifts a megaphone and calls out to the rescuers, lined up in pairs like unchosen pallbearers. "We're all done now, boys," he says. "Nobody here can do no more. Only God can."

Tuesday, August 3, 1915
Waterloo, Iowa
4:40 AM

Bernard Joseph McCarville's inner farmer's clock wakes him as the meager first light of dawn seeps through a single window in the bedroom of his four-room farmhouse. The electrostatic smell of a persistent summer rain is still in the air on the unseasonably cold plains of Northeast Iowa. Bernie is thirty-one years old and does not know that another dawn will not come for him.

He shakes off a patchwork quilt without reaching to his left to see if his wife, Mae, is up. He knows it from the smell of coffee. He splashes water on his face from a white basin, pulls on a blue plaid cotton shirt, snaps up overalls, and puts his feet into brown leather slippers.

He walks the few feet to the kitchen, glancing sideways into the room where four daughters stir; the oldest is six, the youngest still an infant in her rocker-crib.

Mae is in the kitchen, making oatmeal in a large steel pot on the cast iron stove, over a blazing fire of corncobs. Her hair is long, brushed into a flow and tied back with a red kerchief. She smiles and stirs the oatmeal. The coffee has finished boiling in a speckled porcelain pot. Bernie pours a cup, sits on a bench, sheds the slippers, and pulls on rubber boots. He takes the coffee and moves outside into the muddy farmyard and the grayscale day, toward the small barn on his forty-acre leased plot.

Two workhorses, Able and John, have spent the night in the lean-to by the barn. Their damp summer coats shine. Their manes fall thick and coarse. They nicker for breakfast, twitching a bit at the withers. Bernie gives them alfalfa from the haymow and a coffee can each of oats in their feed bags. The horses cannot think of the end of days.

Bernie takes a scolding from a few roosters in the chicken yard as he walks to the hog pen, mud clinging to his boots. The hogs grunt and squeal as he feeds them potato skins, wormy apples from the basement, and table scraps. He makes a mental note of the four hogs that will travel with him, Able, and John in an hour's time.

Bernie goes to the well to pump the day's household water. He primes the pump, then raises its long iron handle up and down. Rain dots the water as it spills into two pails. He carries them to the house, heels off his boots on the porch, and enters to the smell of bacon frying in the kitchen. His daughters are up, rubbing the sleep from their eyes, knowing their father has a trip today. The eldest, Helen Clare, holds her infant sister, Josephine Rita, while the middle two, Agnes Mary and Marjorie, huddle for warmth at the stove in their flannel pajamas. They will eat their breakfast at the same kitchen table on which they were born.

Chicago
6:40 AM

Nathan Williams walks a siding outside the Chicago Rail Yards. He is cold, hungry and standing damaged. He wears dungarees, thin at the knees and belted with a remnant of clothesline. A faded gray shirt and hobnailed boots, worn level to the soles, have stood him well—even through the terrible chores at the *Eastland*'s side.

He badly needs to get to Waterloo. From past experiences hopping empty boxcars, he doesn't like the company of hobos. He knows how to work hard to get what he needs. He has made himself familiar with the Chicago train tables and knows that Illinois Central No. 52 is scheduled to depart on Track 11 in a little more than an hour, pulling nineteen cars of fresh fruit through Eastern Iowa to its final stop in Waterloo.

Nathan locates No. 52's locomotive, a black, twelve-wheeled behemoth already huffing out steam. The boiler lighter has been aboard since dawn, to stoke and bank its firebox, gone cold overnight. Outside, Leroy Townsend is leaning against 52's tender, smoking a tailor-made cigarette. Townsends's blue and white striped cap identifies him as the train's engineer. He gives a cautious nod to Nathan, who returns the gesture with a diffident smile and asks if there is any work to be had for passage to Waterloo—perhaps a job beating his way on the tender.

Townsend looks dismissive, then considers it and calls over to C. H. Parker, the conductor, who is winding a gold-plated Illinois pocket watch and looking down the track at the long line of cars where a crew of men load crate after crate of apples, oranges, bananas and melons. Parker is in a bad mood, grousing to himself.

An hour earlier, a white panel truck had pulled up to a maintenance building alongside Track 11, parallel to No. 52's caboose. Men in coveralls carried two wooden coffins to the caboose, lifting them over its iron railings and into the shiny, wood-paneled compartment, where they occupied its passageway. Parker observed all in anger.

At the tender, Townsend and Parker have a discussion, size up Nathan from a distance, and then motion him over. They tell him they don't usually like to hire "darkies," but they're short a fireman today. They look closely at his arms and shoulders, question his energy and his endurance with a shovel. He "Yassirs" repeatedly to their queries and tells them he can shovel coal faster than any man they'll ever see. Parker tells him that better be true or he'll be tossed at the first stop on the way west.

Waterloo
7:10 AM

Bernie McCarville downs his oatmeal, bacon, and eggs and rises to leave. Mae hands him an apple butter and bacon sandwich wrapped in a dishcloth. She embraces him and whispers something in his ear. He winces, then takes Josephine from Helen and cradles her for a moment as the three others gather around him, begging for peppermint sticks to be brought home from town.

Bernie scrapes mud from his galoshes on the porch and puts them on again. At the barn, he wrestles with secondhand tackle, traded for a dressed-out hog at the Waterloo Saddlery Company. Able and John go willingly out of their hackamores and into harness, as if they sense the outing. Next comes the fifteen-foot lumber wagon, its four twelve-spoked wheels rebanded in springtime. Bernie lifts the sides into place and heaves a ramp onto the back end. Four tagged, ill-fated hogs, protesting loudly, are driven from the pen and pushed up the ramp.

Bernie installs the endgate, climbs to his seat, gathers the reins, and puts the team forward with a wave to Mae, now nursing Josephine, and the other three girls gathered on the porch. Two Lombardy poplar trees mark the farm's boundary on the northeast corner of Donald and Sage Streets, ten miles south of Denver, Iowa, and the slaughterhouse where Bernie will sell the hogs. He gees the team north on Sage and settles in for a three-hour trip to Denver.

The rain has slacked under slate skies, but muddy roads promise a slowed pace—perhaps four miles to the hour.

Sage and Donald
7:35 AM

Mae sees that the girls are dressed, the baby bathed, the dishes washed and dried, and the beds made. She puts on a shawl and goes outside to scatter corn and eggshells for the chickens, then milks the two cows, their udders bulging. Finally, she eats her own breakfast of oatmeal and sliced apples and sits down in her rocker to mend Bernie's socks and a worn spot in his only pair of worsted woolen trousers for Sunday Mass.

Chicago
8:05 AM

Nathan Williams is already sweating in the breezeless tender, his face beginning to sear. The firebox gates open like a clamshell as he loads shovels-full of coal from the tender into its mouth. His actions take on the synchrony of a machine as he fills his shovel from the tender, makes a 180-degree turn, depresses a pedal with his right foot to open the firebox, shifts his weight, and heaves the load into the roaring blaze.

Townsend checks his gauges and pulls some levers. The engine strains, and power goes to the pistons, then the drive wheels. No. 52 sighs a bit and starts its laborious roll. Townsend keeps a close eye on Nathan from his commanding seat up front on the right. One by one, like infantrymen in battle gear, the freight cars obey the transferred energy and roll slowly out of the town that Carl Sandburg named "City of the Big Shoulders" a year ago.

Give or take, it will be nine hours on three hundred miles of track to reach Waterloo, including stops in Rockford and Dubuque. Parker, looking back, assures himself that all cars are riding smooth, then makes his way to the locomotive, still grousing. "Cripes, Leroy, this ain't no manifest train," he says. "It breaks the rules, them being back there. My caboose ain't no hearse."

Townsend looks up from his time sheet. "Geeze, C.H.," he responds, "we gotta think of that *Eastland* sorrow. A whole young family lies back there in them coffins. We owe their kin waiting in Iowa."

Parker submits, puts the subject behind, and begins to brag to Townsend about his new thermos jug—a birthday gift from his wife. He says the coffee in it will still be hot in Waterloo if there's any left.

Denver, Iowa
11:35 AM

Bernie McCarville pulls into Denver's eastern city limits, late by his reckoning, his jacket and sandwich soaked through with a resurgent rain. He'd had to stop twice on the way: once to help push a new Campbell Overland motorcar out of a ditch—its owner nonplussed by the betrayals of modernity—and the second, to right one of the hogs that had lost a contest with a wagon-mate and was collapsed on its side, squealing like tarnation.

Bernie rides into the small farm town, past a few clapboard houses, then a hardware store, a feed store, and three taverns. The steeple of a Lutheran church rises immodestly on the western outskirts, its turret thinning into the still-gray sky. Bernie spots the slaughterhouse, two hundred yards ahead. He is thirsty and impatient now, having spotted the taverns.

A short, heavy man in a bloody white apron comes out at the rear of the slaughterhouse, greets Bernie, and begins to assess the four hogs. They weigh the hogs in at an average of 43 pounds, haggle for the obligatory several minutes, then settle on the previous day's market price of $12.18 per live head. The man lets Bernie hose out waste from the wagon at a side spigot and water Able and John. Then Bernie McCarville, his load and mood lightened, rides away with his $209.96 fortune in cash.

Heading west through town, Bernie selects his next destination. The tavern with the Grain Belt Beer sign in the window beckons a thirsty and successful farmer. Bernie reins up, gets down, shakes out his hat and jacket, and enters. Two farmers sit together at a side table, and one is alone at the bar. Enthused by the surfeit of cash, a roof over his head, and the warmth to come, he picks a stool and orders two mugs of Pabst Blue Ribbon on tap, then asks the man closest to him to pass a big glass jar of pickled eggs. The man complies and introduces himself. Bernie thinks he hears Irish in the surname. They exchange assessments of how bad the rain and cold are for crops and lament the *Eastland* disaster in Chicago and the Iowa couple. Bernie taps glasses with the man and confirms their Irish heritage. He talks of his father, John, born in Ireland in 1854. Bernie looks down at the sawdust floor when his eyes moisten involuntarily as he thinks ambivalently of John McCarville, dead of uremia two years ago in March. There was the loan of seed money from father to son, a failure to pay the debt, a public dressing down, and an insistence on double interest.

Sage and Donald
12:10 PM

Mae McCarville's darning is complete for the time being. She is fussing over Agnes, who has somehow tangled paraffin in her hair from the seal on a jam jar. Agnes blames it on Helen; Helen blames it on Marjorie. May hands Agnes a rosary to distract her and combs out what she can of the paraffin. Out in the sodden pasture, the two cows stand in the grass, chewing their cuds.

Mae considers where Bernie might be at this point and masks her apprehension. Agnes is released, and Mae goes to the icebox to place a moist towel over the dressed chicken for dinner, then retrieves potatoes from the dirt-walled basement and peels and drops them in a pan of cold water. She takes Josephine up and calls the girls together. They recite a familiar prayer:

"Dear Saint Christopher, holy patron of travelers, lead him safely to his destiny. Protect him today in all his travels along the road's way. Give your warning sign if danger is near so that he may stop until the path is clear."

East of Rockford
1:40 PM

C. H. Parker records the train's speed at forty miles per hour. No. 52, white smoke gushing from its blast stack, swoops by an eastbound grain freight relegated to a siding. Nathan Williams is having only his second break, gulping water out of a steel jug with a battered dipper—used by no one else. He looks to Townsend for approval of his work, getting none.

When No. 52 stops at Rockford, Nathan gets off briefly to relieve himself in the "Coloreds Only" privy. He splashes his face from the tap and washes away some grime, wondering how he will find a bath and clean clothes in Waterloo and what else he will find there. He reaches into his back pocket to retrieve the folded postcard received the day before at his tenement rooming house on Twenty-Ninth Street in the "Black Belt" ghetto of Chicago's South Side. The card, now moist with sweat, is written in blunt pencil. It reads, "Fear awful troubles comin' here. Come hep right away." It's signed "Dinah" and postmarked "Waterloo, Iowa, July 26, 1915."

At the Rockford stop, Parker walks back to the caboose, climbs the rear steps, and peers at length through the window at the caskets. His face alters and then softens. He raises his head a bit to the skies and stands erect and still.

As Nathan returns to the tender, a half-dozen people, waiting on the platform for a passenger train, look at him askance. Three of the freight cars are off-loaded within the hour, then C. H. Parker calls "All aboard!"—mostly for show. No. 52 chugs off.

Denver, Iowa
2:50 PM

The Irishmen, in full story mode, have cracked the shells of peanuts and barroom friendship. They order one more round of Pabst. Bernie McCarville, the successful farmer, pays, fingering two dimes and a nickel toward the bartender. Outside, Able and John, bored and dripping with rain, step and quiver in the muddy gravel street. Bernie checks the clock at the end of the bar and thinks he'd better get going. His new friend tells of how his own father arrived at the docks in Boston to see warning signs posted on the wharf: "No Dogs or Irishmen Allowed." They discuss freedom in America and impending war. Finally, the two shake hands and promise to have another meeting down the line. Bernie visits the urinal, goes out to his team and wagon, climbs up, and shakes the reins for Waterloo. He is about to pass the lone grocery store when he stops abruptly, ties up the reins, and enters. A tin Coca-Cola sign in the window boasts, "Relieves Fatigue." Bernie pays quickly for a dozen bottles of Grain Belt and gets a free opener. He hefts the cardboard box to the wagon and mounts and calls the team to attention. Across the street, at the small fire station, men in uniform are polishing an ancient pump truck.

Waterloo
3:25 PM

Sidney D. Smith, MD, the Black Hawk County coroner, records his findings from yesterday's autopsy on the body of a middle-aged black woman, found murdered the night before on a Waterloo street. Smith, a gaunt and severe man of sixty-two, notes the deep knife slashes to the face and torso of the victim's body.

On the last page of the report, Smith pauses over the blank line for the notification of next of kin, checks his notes from the police files, and fills in "Nathan T. Williams, Colored, Chicago, Illinois. Address unknown."

West of Denver, Iowa
4:50 PM

Bernie McCarville, woozy and momentarily serene, lets Able and John set the pace as they continue west, well outside Denver but miles north of Waterloo. Horseradish plants grow randomly along the road and in the ditches. A silo in a farmyard spills last year's corn out of its broken bottom lathes. Two mangy dogs break from a wheat field and run alongside the wagon. In a cornfield off to the right, a farmer tries out his new Waterloo Boy tractor.

Hours later and nearing home, Bernie turns south on Killdeer Road, crosses 270th, and in two miles, reaches Gresham Road. At the intersection, he pauses the team and ponders a melancholy impulse to visit his father's grave. He's been thinking of this since the talk with his new friend in Denver and of his decision two years ago, after John McCarville's funeral Mass, to go elsewhere instead of Calvary Cemetery. He passes a farmhouse with the mailbox painted shiny black, its red flag raised. Bernie decides it's time for reparations.

Sage and Donald
6:40 PM

Mae McCarville sweeps the floors again and strains the morning's milk. She has already been out in the drizzle to hoe the garden, drive the cows in, put down straw in Able and John's stall, and swill the remaining hogs. A spray of fresh bridal wreath is in a yellow clay vase on the kitchen table. Butter is yet to be churned. Bernie should be home soon. She says the prayer again to herself.

Waterloo
7:05 PM

Bernie McCarville, his route suddenly changed, turns Able and John off of Burton Avenue between Gresham and Bennington Streets and into the pilastered gates of Calvary Cemetery. He reins up and opens another Grain Belt, then gets down and walks unsteadily among the chiseled gravestones until he finds the one he wants. An image of his father, atrophied and hallucinating, comes into focus. Bernie stops at his father's marker, begins to weep, then gradually descends into the rage blooming inside him. He smashes the bottle over the stone, and splinters fall like bronze mementoes on John McCarville's grave. Bernie stomps away, sure he made the wrong decision back there at Gresham Road. He collapses against a wagon wheel in dizziness and despair.

No. 52
7:45 PM

Nathan Williams puts his shovel aside and scans the landscape. He is worn-out in every way, drenched in perspiration and eager to leave the cramped tender and its swelter. Townsend and Parker have finished most of the thermos of coffee and are eager too for the various comforts of the city. They see the farmlands flowing past them like a long roll of green crepe narrowing in scope. More and more rail sidings appear on their flanks to manage the seventy-five trains and seventy thousand cars of freight that go in and out of Waterloo every year.

Sage and Donald
8:25 PM

Other farmers are coming in from their fields now, but Mae McCarville is still waiting, worried sick from instinct and experience. She has fed the children and put Bernie's dinner on the stove top in a covered plate: half a chicken, mashed potatoes and string beans. She keeps saying the prayer, over and over.

Waterloo
8:55 PM

Back on the road, Bernie McCarville remembers the gentle admonition Mae whispered to him in the kitchen about his drinking. Another wave of guilt sweeps over him, then doubles down as he suddenly realizes that he forgot to buy peppermint sticks at the grocery in Denver. He lashes the reins on Able and John's haunches, and they quicken into a trot toward home. At the edge of a field to his left, a rusted old thresher lies, the crumpled page of a giant history book, oddly overturned, its tines clawing like a dead beetle.

Bernie reaches Burton Road again and heads south, passing Mount Vernon Road, then Dunkerton Road. The team is tiring and lathered, but he keeps at them.

Still on Burton, they pass Big Rock Road and go the final mile to Donald Street, three hundred yards from Broadway, where the Illinois Central tracks cross. Bernie is now only three miles from home. Inexplicably though, the team doesn't haw to the left on Donald Street but continues south on Burton, away from home, picking up yet more speed. Two farm boys in oversized yellow rain slickers look up from exploring the edge of a cellar hole.

No. 52
8:58 PM

The locomotive is a little more than a quarter mile from the Burton Avenue crossing at Broadway. Townsend slows his speed to fifteen miles per hour, and now pulls a lanyard three times to whistle the standard intersection warning.

Parker begins to stow his thermos in a canvas bag. He pauses, unscrews the cap, and says to Nathan Williams,

"Well, you did okay, boy. Hold out that there dipper."

Nathan complies, and Parker pours the dregs of the coffee for him.

With No. 52's lower speed and the Waterloo Yards nearing, Nathan is able to slack off. He looks out the vertical side opening of the tender and, in the lasting summer light, sees a team of horses and a wagon coming rapidly from the north. As its distance closes, he begins to hear the sound of horse hooves.

Waterloo
8:59 PM

Able and John are running full-out. A stray lilac bush in a culvert sways in the backwash of the wagon. Three box elder trees are still dripping rain. The remaining bottles of beer clink in the cardboard. Bernie is suddenly aware of the gambler's choice before him. The train is long and slow. Bernie is sullen and late. He cracks the reins and swears out to the team, certain that they can cross in time.

Burton Avenue and Broadway
9:01 PM

Bernie McCarville realizes it is too late. He pulls the reins sharply back and to his right. The team, wild-eyed, tries gamely to respond, but there is no time. Both horses crash into the locomotive's side, just ahead of Nathan Williams's position on the tender, where he watches in horror. The momentum thrusts the team forward and into the train's cattle guard. Townsend applies the emergency brake system.

Able's left front hoof shears off at the fetlock. His shoulder compounds and separates from his body at the withers. John attempts to rear to avoid the impact, but he strikes the train full-on, his head and neck crushed by the force. He falls back, instantly dead. Able, keening and pulsing out blood, flails at what remains of the harness, then gives out his last struggle as he drops sideways.

Bernie McCarville catapults twenty feet out of his seat, his arms akimbo, into a forward half-somersault. His left foot catches on the frontpiece of the wagon, fracturing his thigh. Bernie's full body weight slams into Able's hindquarters, rupturing Bernie's gut. Of its own accord, his body hurls forward, shocked and senseless, until his head connects to the roadway, fracturing his skull at the hairline.

The shock of the sudden stop reverberates along the spine of the train cars like a shiver, ending at the caboose. The two coffins jostle slightly. Townsend and Parker scramble down from No. 52 and run to the wreckage. They see the wagon, nearly unmarred by the impact, and sustain hope that its driver is alive. Parker slips on the horses' blood on the tracks as he rushes to Bernie McCarville, who lies askew amid the carnage. Parker bends to look in Bernie's blank eyes, then shakes his head at Townsend.

Nathan Williams walks timidly toward Bernie McCarville, but Parker shushes him back to the tender, where Williams slumps, overcome by death and its forebodings. Instinctively, he retrieves the soaked postcard from his pocket.

Burton and Broadway
9:55 PM

Waterloo police and railroad authorities crowd the scene, which is lit up by flashlights and the headlight beams of fire trucks and police cars. Dr. Sydney Smith, the coroner, is notified at home that a late case is coming in. The doctor is vexed that he'll have to give up another night by the wireless. Two men place Bernie's body on a stretcher, cover it with a white sheet and take it by carriage to the nearby O'Keefe & Towne Funeral Parlors, where Bernie McCarville is identified by a bankbook in the left pocket of his bloody jacket.

Dr. Smith arrives to make his initial examination. He notes, "Fracture of the neck and skull. Rupture of the intestines. Fracture of the left thigh. Dead on impact."

Sage and Donald
11:05 PM

The phone rings three times in quick succession. Mae McCarville, praying in her rocker, rushes to it. Neighbors on the party line leap from their beds and reading lamps to listen in. Mae bunches her rosary into her palm and picks up the receiver on the wall.

"Mae McCarville, wife of Bernard McCarville? Dr. Smith, the coroner. I have your husband down here. Come and get him."

Mae screams and faints. Her elder daughters hover over her in bewilderment while the infant still sleeps.

Thursday, August 5
Saint Joseph's Church, Waterloo
10:00 AM

The hearse from O'Keefe & Towne brings Bernie McCarville's brown wooden casket. Pallbearers carry it to the front of the church for the requiem Mass. Mae is ashen and, for the first time in her adult life, fragile. Helen carries Josephine, while Marjorie and Agnes surround their mother in nascent understanding.

The priest intones, "Thou knowest, Lord, the secrets of our hearts. Shut not thy merciful ears to our prayer, but spare us, Lord most holy, O God most mighty, O holy and merciful Savior, thou most worthy judge eternal, suffer us not, at our last hour, for any pains of death, to fall from Thee."

Forty-four miles north of Waterloo, in New Hampton, a hearse has brought the remains of newlyweds Louise Jahnke, 29, and her husband, Paul, 30, drowned aboard the SS *Eastland*. Relatives and friends of the couple stand by their graves at Graceland Cemetery.

"Both had a dread of the boat," exclaims Mrs. Paul Altman, the couple's landlady and friend. "They were married just six weeks. Mrs. Jahnke was fussing over the lunch the day before they left—when she stopped and expressed fear that something would happen on the boat."

The huddle of mourners shifts eyes toward her.

"Now they are dead," she says. "Mr. Jahnke rang my bell the day they left. 'Here is my key and the fifty dollars for my mother if we don't come back from the trip,' he said."

Inside the Jahnkes' flat, on the bedroom dresser, relatives will find a will and a letter in Louise Jahnke's cursive hand. She wished that her mother might have her bracelet and rings.

Calvary Cemetery
1:15 PM

Mae and the children stand under a dark-green awning, disconsolate. Fresh Iowa soil, black and fecund as the coal in No. 52's firebox, is banked up beside Bernie's grave like the remnant of a forgotten furrow. The priest's purple stole flutters in a light westerly breeze as he circles the casket, murmuring Latin. The semisweet scent of incense drifts around the grim mourners: farmers and their wives; C. H. Parker, in his dress railroad uniform; and an Irish farmer from Denver.

Thirty yards away, at the fringes of Calvary, yet another burial service has concluded. A sole mourner is walking away from the grave of his sister and toward the tent sheltering the remains of Bernie McCarville. He wears a laundered shirt, dungarees, and worn hobnailed boots. He whispers a question to John Hogan, the O'Keefe & Towne funeral director. Hogan nods curtly.

The man waits tentatively for the priest to finish. As the small crowd disperses, he approaches the casket where Mae and the children still stand, struggling to cope. Mae notices him and turns toward him. "Yes, sir?" she says.

"Missus McCarville," Nathan Williams whispers, "I saw your husband at the last. I'm awful sorry, ma'am. I figure he was goin' fast to come home to you."

Epilogue

Mae and Bernie McCarville, whose graves lie beside each other at Calvary Cemetery, were the grandparents of the author and his eight siblings. The second daughter, Agnes Mary, was their mother. The life and whereabouts of Nathan Williams after August 3, 1915 are thus far untraceable.

Tim Hurley, the author's brother, provided extensive research for this story. He served three times as mayor of Waterloo and is a lifelong civic and business leader of the Cedar Valley community.

The Second Drawer Revolver

Sometimes I act a lot older than I am.
—Holden Caulfield

I have to warn you right away, I talk a lot—even for fourteen. My grandma says I must have been vaccinated with a phonograph needle. "Good gravy!" she says when I'm going on and on.

Anyway, I've been thinking a lot about what happened two months ago. My new doctor told me I should try writing it all down, so here goes.

Damn good. That's how I would say it felt to be alone in the house for once—with my mom and dad and little brother, Billy, gone out to Aunt Marge's for supper and all the talk and everything that naturally goes with that kind of affair. I didn't know why they left me home. It was okay, though. This is 1950, and I'm *fourteen,* for God's sake. But I think the reason was, there was trouble someplace. I can smell trouble.

Channel 8 was coming in clear for the first time in days. Usually, there were *huge* amounts of snow. I was enjoying the heck out of my favorite detective show. I guess they must have put up a higher tower over at Channel 8 or at least something to help things out because this show had never come in that good before. None of the other two dumb bunny stations around here ever carried this one show I was

---

19

watching, so I always had to revert to good old Channel 8 over in Waterloo, about five miles from the place I live.

We haven't had TV for long. My dad got us an Admiral with a sixteen-inch screen. We couldn't believe it when they delivered it. I heard my mom saying we couldn't afford it—that we needed coal. Later, my dad got an electric thing with a colored wheel that goes around and acts like color TV. Completely phony.

I remember two years ago when I saw my first TV. I used to deliver the newspaper on my horse. I had this delivery bag with front and back sides. After you fold your papers, you're supposed to put it over your head and go walking on delivery. But I turned it into saddlebags for the horse, which was pure genius.

I'd ride up in front of the houses and toss a paper right on a front porch. Of course, if I missed, which was rare, I'd get down and go get it. I take care of my customers. Anyway, one night in winter when it was dark as hell, I was finishing my route. At this one customer's house, I saw a funny light through the front window, flickering. I put the horse a little closer and stood up in the stirrups, and what the hell, I saw my first TV. I found out it was a show called *Captain Video*.

Waterloo is a big city, and they always show this detective story. Sometimes narrow-minded people in charge of big cities, you know, don't show great stuff. That's them all right—*never* showing anything worth it. Just that drab highbrow stuff like opera and *Omnibus* and *Wide Wide World*, Garroway's show. The comedian fella Steve Allen says, and I agree, it should be *Big, Fat, Greasy, Slimy Old World*. My dad *loves* Dave Garroway. What does that tell you? Allen is one of the few grown-ups who has it on the ball.

To get back to what I was saying, I was really having a good time of it. Had a cold beer beside me too—a Schlitz—and a ham sandwich that my mom made me. Had a pack of smokes too, right on the table next to the sofa—Chesterfields, which I lifted from the back seat of my dad's Nash. Nothing like a good supply of cigs, you know—especially when you don't have a ten-year-old brother by the name of Billy in your hair all the time. Not that I hate my brother. It's just that the little shit bugs me at various times—always running around the house when a guy wants to watch a good show, like the one on Channel 8.

My dad is a traveling salesman, and my mom takes care of us and bakes bread and sweet rolls for church sales—I mean, *all* the time. My dad is usually home only on weekends. Sometimes he comes home really late on Fridays and isn't himself, as my mom says. My mom has us go to bed early those nights.

Billy and I sleep downstairs. His feet smell to high heaven. One Friday night two months ago, when my dad wasn't himself, everybody had gone to bed. My dad was talking so loud upstairs, it woke me up. I could hear my mom's little voice, and she was scared. Then I heard her yell, and she fell down the stairs. It's confusing as hell when your mom falls down the stairs and you don't fight or cry.

I have to apologize for cussing. My dad won't allow it, but then he says stuff like *gaddang* and *shite* and *chicken-s*—I say, say it all or nothing at all, but I watch myself around so-called grown-ups.

Anyway, the thing I don't like most about kids is that they never sit still. Always running around and doing something—never want to relax and enjoy the nicer facts of life. Besides, if Billy would have been home that night, or my mom and dad, I would've never been drinking my beer, or relaxing with a smoke. I figure a man is old enough to smoke and drink beer when he's fourteen, but they sure don't. Another thing I don't like about kids is the way they tattle everything. Billy is an awful tattletale, any way you look at it, and he would tell on me if he caught me smoking or drinking. That's just not honorable.

I need to explain just how much of a guy Billy is—tattlewise. I want that to be known. One time, I was messing around in the chest of drawers in the dining room, not looking for anything especially, and I saw Dad's gun in the second drawer, where he's ordinarily kept it—ever since I've been a kid, let alone since Billy's been a kid.

Anyway, it's an admirable firearm. A six-shooter, you'd call it, if you're one of those who watch the Matt Dillon sort of thing on TV. I generally don't since detective stories are my favorites, and I don't go for those westerns with what they call a weak plot. That's what my English teacher used to say before I was kicked out of school. She said all those western soap shows had weak plots. I agree with her.

But let's get on with the example. I was just standing there, admiring that revolver and twirling the cylinder once or twice, when this brother of mine comes into the dining room and sees me. Well, I will tell you—a normal person would've thought a cyclone had come. The house was falling in—walls and all—the way that kid carried on, ranting and yelling to my mom about me having that gun out.

My dad had instructed us kids never to touch that gun unless he was with us under any circumstances—no matter what they were. My mom hated that gun, but my dad said it was there to teach us a lesson. There I was, just messing around and not hurting a soul—much less Billy, and he acted like I was taking potshots at my mom's best china.

Well, did I ever catch it that night from my dad. He made me go out and cut a switch from a tree and take it to the garage. He waited awhile and then came out. He didn't seem to like doing it, but he had a funny look on his face. He said that's what his dad did. Damn him. I shouldn't be cussing my grandpa. He's been dead for three years, and as my mom says, he's in heaven and hence able to help us folks get there too. But no matter where my grandpa is, or anyone else, I just wanted to show how much of a tattler Billy is.

By the way, I'm a pretty straight shot with my own gun, my Daisy Red Ryder BB rifle. I've even taken Billy out to the woods with me a few times and let him shoot at old beer cans and other stuff—even if he's too young yet. I always try to be a good brother. That's probably why I'm so pissed that Billy always tells on me.

To get back to my main story, I was sitting there on the sofa with my feet up on the hassock, eating my sandwich, and watching the tube when all of a sudden, somebody knocked on the back door. I didn't have an idea in the world who it could be, so I put my shoes back on and kind of stuffed my shirt in a little so as to look presentable and stashed the beer and cigs.

It turned out that it was a guy I didn't know who rang the doorbell. He wanted to use the phone to call his wife to come and get him. He said he ran out of gas down the road on his way home from Waterloo, where he worked. I told him he was welcome to use the phone. I'm a good person that way.

He said thanks a lot and that he was sure much obliged even though he was mad that he had run out of gas. He didn't *seem* really mad though. He seemed something else. I got that sense of trouble but not as bad as I should have.

I showed him the hallway where the phone is and went back into the living room, you know, to give him privacy. I respect privacy and wish Billy did. Well, he proceeded to pick up the phone and dial a few numbers, while I was sitting there, more or less relaxing again.

I thought there was something a bit phony about the whole thing though since he didn't seem to be letting the little wheel on the phone come back around to where it belongs before you dial the next number. I got to thinking that he really wasn't dialing any particular address at all. You get that kind of thing from detective shows.

And it turned out that I was right. He had just pretended to talk to his wife on the phone so as to get me off guard, and after all that fake crap, he hung up the phone, and I saw him walk nonchalantly over to me with a gun in his hand.

Remember how good I was telling you that show on Channel 8 was? After this guy showed up in front of me, I kind of forgot all about the TV, if you take my meaning. Well, this guy was about six feet tall and dressed all ritzy and everything, and he had a sneer on him that you've never seen. I've seen a better sneer on a coyote. The guy looked as near as if he wanted to hurt somebody as you've ever seen any human look—male or female.

It was kind of funny that, except for a shorter barrel, his gun was pretty near exactly like the Second Drawer Revolver. That's the name I had for my dad's gun. These two guns being alike just points out to you how coincidences can take place at the oddest times. That tells you something.

Well, I was gut-punched by what had taken place—much more by how quickly it had all happened. Another funny thing is, this guy didn't talk very much at all, considering how high-toned he acted. He just told me to hand over all the money and jewelry we had around the house.

I don't personally have any money or jewelry myself. Plus, my dad doesn't make much these days. I told this guy that, but he smiled and straightened out the arm holding the gun. I don't mind telling you that by this time, I was getting more riled up. I kept telling him that I didn't know where in the heck the money was kept—if indeed there was any money in the house. But he just didn't want to take no for an answer. He said he knew goddamn well this was Billy's house and there was money and jewelry. He cocked the revolver. Now, we all know this is not *Billy's* house. But you think I was gonna correct him? *Hell no.*

So I started forming a little plan about how I could get him off my back. I don't want to brag, but this will prove that I know how to handle myself. It came into my mind that my dad's gun was sitting in the dining room—in that chest of drawers—and doing nothing. So I went ahead and told the guy that okay, okay, my dad had a whole bunch of silver dollars and my grandpa's gold railroad watch in that chest of drawers in the dining room. Sometimes you have to lie in an emergency. The gold-watch part was true though.

In the final interpretation though, this guy must not have been too smart because he fell for my plan. He must've thought I was just a kid. He followed me real persnickety-like to the dining room and stood by the china closet.

Well, I started giving him some of the phony crap that he had done to me with the phone. I acted like I was looking in the second drawer for the silver dollars. When my hand felt the handle of the Second Drawer Revolver, I felt relieved. I used the tablecloth over the gun to hide the sound of me cocking it. That was smart.

It ended up that I broke some of my mom's best china after all. All of a sudden, I couldn't think about anything except that I knew this was the trouble I had felt coming. I pulled the gun out of the second drawer and shot at his stomach. Close range, it's called.

I'm getting to the end now. The guy's tie went up in the air a little, and he looked surprised at first. I'd never seen anybody look that way. He fell back against the china cabinet, and his shirt got red right away. My ears were ringing really bad, and I felt like I was going to pass out. I put the gun back in the second drawer. It felt like that was the right thing to do.

I went to the phone and knew I had to dial the operator. My finger slipped the first time, and it didn't go all the way around. The operator told me to go out of the house right away and wait for the police. She wanted Aunt Marge's number, which I gave her from memory. I have a pretty good memory.

By this time, the neighbors had come running over, and I could see them in the porch light. Mrs. Watters came in and hugged me and asked if I was all right. Then came the sirens and flashing lights of the police and ambulance. Next, I saw my dad and mom and Billy pull up. They didn't even close the doors of the Nash. They ran up to me, their eyes all scared. I was shaking bad.

The police were all over the place. The first two had their guns out when they came in, but then they put them away. I told them where the Second Drawer Revolver was.

Some people came in after a while and put the guy on a stretcher and covered him up. They took him out the front door—the opposite of how he came in. There's a trellis on that side of the house, and in the flashing lights, I could see some flowers hanging down from it. I wasn't supposed to be watching, but that made me feel bad.

A little later, Mrs. Watters and her husband came in and helped my mom clean up. I could hear them squeezing out a mop and sweeping up the china pieces. Nobody went into the dining room for a long time after that.

Mrs. Watters is an awfully kind person. One time, she even came over to help us bury our dog. The dog was a collie. A car hit him out in front; it took his nose almost clean off. It was bad. My mom was getting groceries, so she wasn't home. Mrs. Watters got a blanket from her own house and wrapped the collie in it. She let Billy and me help carry it, and we buried it down where the horse grazed. I have to tell you, we were all crying.

Back to where I was. After a while, the police left, and then my dad did something that surprised me. He'd never done it before. I was sure that after all of this—you know, touching the Second Drawer Revolver, letting the guy in, the beer and cigs, the china, and so on—that I was gonna have to go cut a switch—I mean, a *big* switch.

But my dad knelt down on the floor and told me to look at him. He held out his hand to shake mine. My dad had been a football player in high school, and believe me, he had strong hands. He told me I had courage and he was proud of me. I never heard his voice like that. My mom and Billy were watching, and they came over and kept hugging me and crying a lot.

The next morning, two detectives came to the house and talked to my mom and dad in the kitchen. My mom gave them coffee and her cinnamon rolls, which they lapped up. To me, they didn't look like detectives, but then the guy didn't look like a crook at first either. There you go.

Anyway, later on, my mom was still in the kitchen, and I came in and asked her, number one, what the detectives said and number two, why I got left at home. You can usually get the straight skinny from your mom when you get her alone.

I remember that when I woke up on the morning after, I could still smell the gunpowder in my nose. Now I smelled the cinnamon rolls. She wiped her hands on her apron and put on some Pacquin's, which I like the smell of.

She sat down close to me and told me Aunt Marge had called her and told her that a woman who was working at the Dairy Queen had seen Billy in a fight outside. The woman had gone to high school with Aunt Marge, so they were friends. The woman told my aunt that one of the kids was hassling Billy about us being a poor family and that our dad was never home and was probably gonna leave for good. My mom was talking very softly, telling this.

The kid kept ragging on Billy, she said, telling him he was an orphan and probably a bastard. Well, Billy took a swing at this other kid and called him the same thing. Billy told the kid what he was saying was bullshit. Billy used that word, and so did my mom. Billy said that our dad had hundreds of silver dollars at the house and bought my mom a hell of a lot of rings and jewelry.

Now, we all know that's not true, so Billy was lying. There's no question about that. But you have to hear the rest of it.

My aunt Marge's friend went out in front of the Dairy Queen and broke up the fight. She said the last thing this kid told Billy was that he was gonna tell his own dad and his dad would prove Billy was a liar and a bastard. Naturally, this woman knew who Billy was, but she didn't know the other kid, so she asked him where he lived. The kid said, "Waterloo."

The detectives told my mom and dad that a warrant had been put out on this kid's dad two days before and that he had been embezzling from his company—whatever that is, but I know it's cheating. They said something about a Ponzi scheme, I think. The right term for that warrant is what we call an APB—an all-points bulletin. What the guy had, besides a gun, is what you call motive.

Anyway, they found out the kid did tell his dad about what Billy said, and that's why his dad showed up that night and knocked on our door. The detectives said the guy was driven by desperation. That's one way to describe it.

My mom and dad didn't take me with them to Aunt Marge's so they could confront Billy and get the truth from him about why he lied. I guess they just wanted to keep me out of it or maybe protect me.

Anyway, I got up from the kitchen table then and went looking for Billy. I found him in the chicken yard, throwing pebbles at the roosters and crying. I went up to him and knelt down in the chicken yard and told him to look at me. I said I was proud of him for sticking up for our dad and told him it was courage and that sometimes you have to lie to be true. I really felt like his big brother, doing this.

My dad told everybody I must have had what's called an intuition that night. I didn't know you could have that at fourteen.

This whole story tells you two things: One, you shouldn't cheat anybody or lie about running out of gas. People, even kids, can sense a lie if they watch decent detective shows. Two, it's easier to shoot somebody than to get over shooting somebody. Also, stay away from opera.

One thing I almost forgot to put in is about beer and cigs. If you're a kid and your mom has a nose with a range of fifty yards, you have to have a pack of Sen-Sens handy. It's essential. Sen-Sen is little black squares that taste a lot like strong licorice. If somebody's coming, you pop a couple in and—*Shazam!*—no beer or cig smell. It's a miracle. I forgot the Sen-Sen that night. Be sure you always have it—you know, for emergencies.

An earlier version of "The Second Drawer Revolver"
appeared in The Spokesman *(Fall 1958).*
Gilbert Keith Chesterton Award for Short Story, Loras
College, 1959.

II

Memoirs

I say, bury the work in its old clothes,
let's go inside to learn how fire lives on top of ashes and watch
how shadows of light
leap to the windows.

—James Hearst

A Personal Rebuke
from Robert Frost

Sleet, that pesky half brother of rain and snow, threads together recollections of young life in northeastern Iowa. Sleet, on the gray casket of our monsignor and on my starched white altar-boy surplice as his mortal remains were blessed, then carried away from Saint Joseph's in Waterloo.

Sleet, tap-tapping the bent head of my horse and me as we delivered the *Cedar Falls Daily Record,* keeping a frigid but sacred pact with customers and the journalism fraternity.

And sleet scoured the windows of the publication office at Loras College on a late February afternoon in Dubuque in 1959, when the phone rang at the editor's desk of *The Spokesman,* the college's literary magazine.

I picked up to find Father Raymond Roseliep, the quarterly's faculty advisor, on the line. "You and Tom better come over later," he said with a tone of secrecy.

"Tom" was Tom Ryan—my coeditor, fellow senior writing student, and a Marine veteran of the Korean War. He had an enviable weekend job as a reporter at the *Freeport Journal-Standard* in nearby Illinois.

Ryan and I made an unlikely pair: he was a man who could talk of foreign lands and their off-duty seductions and, of machine-gun emplacements and enemy troops dying north of the Thirty-Eighth

Parallel and me, barely twenty-one, whose farthest travel had been three hundred miles to visit an aunt in a convent and who had killed only garter snakes out of fear and chickens for dinner.

Moreover, Ryan seemed like a fellow already sure of his goal to be a journalist, while I had already been dismissed from a nearby seminary for irreligious hijinks and for attending my meditation in an impaired, drunken condition. I had wrongly viewed the priesthood as an obligatory vocation, thrown up my breakfast daily, and had no authentic career objective except to follow a nascent urge to write.

On the other hand, Raymond F. Roseliep, PhD, 42, had excelled. He was one of the leading priest-poets of his generation. His work appeared regularly in *Four Quarters, Chicago Review, The Commonweal*, and other leading journals. Roseliep's first hardbound volume, *The Linen Bands* (1961), includes many poems that I and other students close to Roseliep had read on onionskin drafts in the seats near the maroon easy chair where he wrote. He was a loving mentor, a devoted friend, and a detailed and demanding editor. In his own work, he was just then beginning to step from earned comfort in traditional lyrical poetry to the ancient soil of haiku. In the years to come, critics would call him the John Donne of Western haiku and the contemporary master of the exacting Japanese form.

Our locale of Dubuque was called Little Rome for its seven hills and plentiful Catholics. The Loras campus was at the top of one of the hills. As a first-year seminarian, I had burned a hole in my windbreaker with the embers of a railroad flare during a nighttime campus rally for John F. Kennedy. Robert Frost would read poetry at Kennedy's inauguration.

With the sleet crackling outside, Ryan and I had been reviewing submissions for our spring issue of *The Spokesman*. Due largely to Roseliep's leadership and notoriety, the quarterly had gained a reputation as an outlet for established poets, essayists, and fiction writers whose works underpinned the magazine's main purpose of showcasing Loras's student writers.

Ryan and I, in our second year as editors, had lofty editorial standards. We once rejected a Loras freshman's poetry submission as "promising but not yet fully developed." The author was David Rabe, who would go on to national prominence, winning Tony and New York Drama Critics' Circle awards for playwriting.

We guessed Roseliep's mysterious call might turn out to be a submission long sought from a major outside poet we had been trying to attract to *The Spokesman*. Greatly intrigued, we wrapped up our work and decided how we would get to Roseliep's quarters on the second floor of the faculty residence a quarter mile away, in a sleet storm.

The direct way was down Loras Boulevard, a steep incline that in foul weather resembled the approach to a giant ski jump. The walking route would cut darkly and circuitously across the campus. We chose the softer way in Tom's '57 Ford convertible, in robin-egg blue to match his wife's eyes. We scraped the windshield, schussed down the slope in low gear and slid into a rare, generous parking spot across from the building.

Roseliep greeted us, cigar in hand. We could always smell its richness in the hallway. He had laid out the usual fare for our frequent editorial conferences: Dubuque Star beers, Hi-Ho crackers, and smoked oysters in metal tins with a slotted opener soldered to the bottom. Toothpicks served as utensils.

Immediately we prodded our advisor for the breaking news. But Roseliep was skilled at cadence and suspense. He talked about the sleet, expressed affection for Tom's wife, and spoke glowingly of Mary Helen Sanders, a young poet and the editor of our sister quarterly at nearby Clarke College. Roseliep, ever the matchmaker, was plotting to introduce me to her. Soon, we met, fell in love, and later married. In 1963, we had a daughter, christened Julia Rose in Roseliep's honor.

Ryan and I finally egged Roseliep into it. He reached to the table beside his writing chair and held up a monarch-sized letter. It was from Paul Engle, founder and vaunted head of the Iowa Writers Workshop at the University of Iowa.

"Gentlemen," Roseliep announced, "get out your finery. We are going to meet Robert Frost."

At first, we thought he was speaking in metaphor. Even though we saw ourselves as worldly, the gap between where Ryan and I were sitting and personal contact with the four-time winner of the Pulitzer Prize was far greater than the distance between Iowa and Frost's New England. Our sense of possibility was overclouded by limits. Still, we could tell Roseliep was serious. By late evening, convinced by the repeated back-and-forth about Engle's letter and the assurances of beer, oysters, and a toast or two of Ballantine's scotch, we called it a night. After kneeling as always to receive Father's blessing, Ryan and I left him for our apartments in the neighborhood.

I was energized and didn't sleep right away. I remembered when I had first encountered Frost's poems in high school. I wasn't studious by any stretch and was often caught looking out the window. But a sophomore teacher, Sister Mary Saint Denise, introduced our class to "Stopping by Woods on a Snowy Evening"—the entry point to Frost for millions of high schoolers. Somehow, the flow of the lines and the story under them caught me looking out the window again, but in a different way. I received a small collection of Frost's poems that Christmas and read it twice before New Year's.

I remembered my second year in seminary in 1956; I had an indelible experience after quoting Frost in Language and Literature class, taught by Rev. James J. Donahue, PhD.

Father Donahue was an emaciated figure. He could not have weighed more than 110 pounds on his tremulous frame. We would see him, badly hungover, struggle into the little coffee shop in Keane Hall, order the soup of the day, and carry it haltingly in his palsied hands to a table, where he often spilled it.

Each time I saw this, a haunting sense of identity came over me. It was not a ghost, as it turned out, but the coming of one.

There was an unconfirmed rumor that Donahue wrote short stories of the Old West under a pseudonym. Rumor aside, he was thought of as a brilliant scholar, and a widely recognized expert on Chaucer.

what he meant by saying that to write poetry is brave. Twisting a newspaper in his hands, Frost said that his original remark had been misunderstood. "To do anything in the arts is brave. You are pitied by your neighbors, you know." He said a woman had once told him that it was sad to be brave. "I replied that it was sadder because it takes brains."

After questions from a self-described beatnik and a science professor, I raised my hand again and asked why Frost always refused to explain his poems. This query was responded to with a cold glare. Engle, sensing the irritation, said "He already did" and went on to the next upward hand. Meanwhile, I was being elbowed by Ryan, the reporter. "He didn't explain *why* though," he whispered. "Don't let him get away with that! Ask it again." I was caught, fearful of both options now facing me.

Eventually, I caught Engle's eye and raised a hand to timid half-staff. Engle, although clearly still uncomfortable at the prospect, pointed again. "Mr. Frost," I intoned through false courage, "I apologize if I didn't make my earlier question clear. Please tell us why you won't explicate your poems."

This time, Frost was ready, or maybe he had been ready all along, but had quivered the arrow. The eyes hardened, his voice rose to its shrillest level of the day, and the response was perfection:

"What do you want me to do? Say it in worse English?"

This surgical strike had the effect of making a magpie into a mute. I fell silent, my face reddened, and my eyes averted downward.

"Way to go," Ryan whispered, but it didn't help much.

Ninety minutes after he had begun, Frost was still going strong, responding to a reporter's request for a definition of his art. "Poetry that which is lost out of prose and verse when translated," he said.

Another reporter had asked earlier if poetry is "contradictions that make sense," to which Frost agreeably replied, "Yes, that too might be a good definition."

Engle, probably protective of Frost's energies, called a halt to the proceedings. The crowd applauded politely and dispersed.

One day, midway through class, Donahue challenged us on poetry. From his chair behind the desk on a riser, he instructed us to close our textbooks and recite from memory our favorite lines.

As others responded, I was dithering. *What should I say to show an advancing intellect? Something pathetic, maybe? Milton on his blindness? Or, with a stroke of boldness, that sinful Keats on his mistress, Fanny Brawne? But I haven't committed any of that to memory!*

When it was my turn, I could bring only Frost to mind: "Whose woods these are, I think I know / His house is in the village though / He will not see me stopping here / To watch his woods fill up with snow." I tacked on an unwise interpretation of who must have owned the woods.

The last student testified, then someone asked, "Now, Father, what are your favorite lines?" Donahue stared at the questioner, then slumped and seemed to change emotionally.

We were anticipating some verses from an obscure work by Chaucer, possibly with a related backstory of being sparked by a long-ago professor of his own.

He got up with great difficulty, stepped gingerly off the riser, and went to a window. The blinds were closed to the afternoon sun. He lifted a fluttering hand to the slats and opened his fingers in a few of them. The light came in on his face, and we could see him blink and the tears coursing. There was a pale luminosity in his eyes. He shifted more toward us, and then the withered old priest began to sing:

"I remember the night, and the Tennessee Waltz. / Now I know just how much I have lost. Yes, I've lost my little darling . . ." He couldn't go on.

Three years later, the day for meeting Robert Frost came as ploddingly as a child's wait for Christmas. On April 13, 1959, five of us embarked for Iowa City: Roseliep, Ryan, Chuck Lorenz, Patrick Johannes, and me.

It was eighty-five miles from Dubuque to Iowa City. No train went between the two points, and we considered a Greyhound too undistinguished for the purpose. We went by car—Roseliep, Ryan, and I in the Ford. There was a six-pack of beer and a bottle of Old

Grand-Dad, procured by an anonymous source from across the Iowa-Illinois border in East Dubuque. Beer had a higher alcohol content there, and merchants had a lower threshold for carding.

Our contingent arrived at the University of Iowa campus in the early afternoon—on time and in requisite dress. We were to meet Engle, our host, in one of the World War II Quonset huts dotting the grounds. They had been built to accommodate the postwar rush of veterans attending on the GI Bill. Engle had granted us access to a small daytime gathering with Frost in advance of his appearance that evening at the university's Memorial Union, which drew an audience of two thousand.

A native of Cedar Rapids, Engle was iconic to us and to those many writers who had advanced under his care at the Iowa Writers Workshop—the creative incubator for such noted talents as John Irving, Robert Bly, Wallace Stegner, and Raymond Carver. Engle contributed poetry and essays to *The Spokesman* and wrote me the next May to compliment the magazine. "You are doing a good job," he ended, probably not knowing how much that modest praise meant to me.

We sat down a few rows back amid some local reporters and a grouping of professors mixed with some past and present students from Engle's classes. Everyone was trying to look studious or detached. Some latecomers had to sit on the floor. We were all smoking.

Robert Frost and Engle entered the room, its windows nailed shut against weather and age. Eight-five years old, Frost moved with a mild iambic shuffle. He removed a high-crowned gray felt hat. A navy tie, featuring red and white circles that offset a white shirt, was tied too short and poked out like an actor from the curtain of his charcoal suit. Polished, black-cap toe shoes completed the ensemble.

His face had wonderful mistakes—the nose designed with oval nostrils and a steep upward slant, its bridge spanning the shores of pale, blue, color-blind eyes below brows shaped like hung parentheses. His white hair looked like it had been cut with a bowl. His ears were oversized shells for salting away sounds.

"I hear everything I write. All poetry is to me first a matter of sound."

He was the most famous man most of us had ever met. There was something separate that drew us to this temporal deity—something buoyant and highly kinetic. Engle had written a chapbook of new poems to commemorate Frost's visit:

"We give this man the sort of praise / we give to ripened autumn days." And, "On this wind-rounded world the bare / Loved face hangs like a bruise in air / We lift our hands to touch it there."

"Hi," Frost said. "Do you know what 'Hi' means? It's 'How are ya?' all run together!"

We were immediately put at some ease. Engle—in rumpled khakis, blue shirt, and tan sport coat—pulled up an armchair for Frost, who immediately declined it, saying, "I might stand to see them." And stand he did—for an hour and a half, holding forth on a wide variety of topics.

About his own notoriety, he said, "People know me throu[gh] television, not my books." But while traveling in Florida recently acknowledged he had not been recognized at all, probably becau[se] his hat. Someone had thought he was a cattleman, which he l[iked] but he declared he would "prefer to be taken for a baseball pit[cher]

Frost delved into his role as the poetry consultant to the Lib[rary of] Congress, having famously complained to the press that his [post] was serving no purpose. "The sign on my door read, 'Cons[ultant in] Poetry.' I thought I was a poetry consultant in everythin[g. I was] mad because nobody consulted me. The blame for all tha[t is mine."

He diverted to the efficacy of prayer, raising at least t[he interest] of the five from Dubuque. "In Congress," he said, "t[here is a] ruling that each session be started with a prayer for per[manent peace.] What's the use of talking about peace? We're bor[n into] conflict. There is no such thing as permanent peace."

Emboldened by this perceived affront, I was n[ow raising] my hand for a question. I had been preassigned b[y Engle to] address Frost. Engle pointed to me, and for a sof[t

Engle made sure that our Loras group had some personal time with Frost to shake his hand and thank him. There is a photo of us with Frost and Engle. I am sitting in the armchair next to Frost, to his left. Our arms are touching—something I was not conscious of at the time but have appreciation for now. Frost has a smile that says he is pleased with himself. I'm smoking and laughing about something Frost had just said to me *sotto voce* about the photographer's shirt and the impermanence of flashbulbs.

I was disconsolate as we walked to the Ford, sure that I had come off as stupid or, worse yet, impertinent. The other four poured balm in my ear, calling my actions pure courage and a brave insistence in pursuit of full truth, or something like that. It worked, and we sailed back to Dubuque on the breezes of our experience, stopping somewhere for hamburgers and malts. No matter when, where, or how Roseliep, Ryan, and I connected afterward, we would always recall Iowa City and the experience of being beside one of the twentieth century's principal American dancers in the art that John Logan called "a ballet for the ear."

Roseliep had been by far the determining influence in my growing confidence that I could write poems and other things. Unforgettable proximities to Frost, Engle, John Logan, Allen Ginsberg, James Hearst, and other poets provided further impetus. My work had already appeared in *Catholic World*, two anthologies, and of course, *The Spokesman*. At Loras, I was given the Gerard Manley Hopkins Award for poetry and the Gilbert Keith Chesterton Award for short story. I felt that, no matter how I made a living in the future, I would always write.

A week before our senior year ended, Roseliep sounded an intuitive note of doubt on the topic. We were sitting alone in his study to talk about marriage and career. He was lighting his cigar, and without context, he said, "What I worry about is not that you won't write, but that you won't write poetry." The prediction would be largely accurate until I finished my business career in 2017.

Ryan and I graduated that June. We parted with Roseliep and each other in tears more open and copious than we wanted. Ryan and his wife moved to California, where he became a crime reporter for the *Santa Monica Outlook*. We would reunite out there in two years and had an unbreakable friendship for life. He succumbed to dementia in 2017.

Father Roseliep—who, much to his liking, we called Spider for his poetic weavings and lanky frame—died in 1983 of an aneurysm. The fatal arrhythmic onset came unpoetically—in his dentist's chair. He is buried in Dubuque in the hand-carved rosewood coffin that he ordered in advance and used as storage for his manuscripts. On his gravestone are carved the first words of his memorial poem to his mother: "Against the Night."

I have not taken the dubious pleasure of smoked oysters from a tin since those many banquets in Roseliep's study. But beer, Ballantine's, and their many cousins are another matter. By the midsixties, aided by genetics from both sides of my family and the insistence of an undeveloped emotional maturity, alcohol was corroding the terminals of thought and action. Fortuitous experience had made me a better writer for wages, but poetry and other ambitions had stalled or receded, and personal ideals were pilfered.

In late 1972, now riven by illnesses and confronted with a crisis that I could no longer postpone or evade, I landed in intensive care at a Los Angeles hospital—a scant 116 pounds and perishing. A man came to my bedside—a Catholic priest who was unknown and unbidden—and said he thought he might know what my problem was. He had experienced it himself and told me that if I was willing to work hard, he would be glad to share the solution with me. What a Roseliep poem calls "a wand of light" came involuntarily to my blacked-out consciousness. I have not had a drink since.

Eleven months later and getting healthier, I came home one evening in February 1974 to hear a message that my father himself was dying in intensive care, in Iowa. A victim of numerous heart attacks at only 59, he was plundered by smoking, alcohol, and overwork. I booked a red-eye to Iowa, changing planes in Chicago. When the flight stopped briefly in Dubuque, heavy snow had begun falling. In the air again and heading toward Waterloo, the storm became blinding and turbulent. I lost any perspective of the ground and then was struck with a dull sureness that I was going to be too late. James W. Hurley had died.

My five brothers and three sisters, individually magnificent, and my mother, that irrepressible matriarch of consolation, formed an iron framework of mutual support. I remember gaining strength against the fear of losing it. Five days later, I was packing for Los Angeles with dual securities: the evergreen and anchoring power of my family and heartland and the hope and stability I knew west of it.

Caught in a sudden moment of reverie, I browsed the small shelf of books in my old bedroom. Hiding between larger volumes was the slim chapbook of Frost poems I had been given for Christmas long ago. I read "Stopping by the Woods on a Snowy Evening," and thought of a note sent by the poet John Logan after I visited his home in 1958 and forgot my notebook. "When you leave something behind," he wrote, "it means you want to come back."

In my mother's kitchen a few minutes later, I looked outside to see sleet. Except for a day in 1961 as a Navy journalist on assignment on a destroyer in the Chesapeake Bay, I had not seen sleet since the day fifteen years earlier when I learned I would meet Robert Frost.

I left my coat and gloves on a chair and went out, slipping a little on the porch steps, and walked under the arbors where my mother's honeysuckle vines would flower again in a few months. I remember an impulse to raise my face to the sleet. A dozen more steps and I could see the small pasture where my brothers and I dug forts in wartime summers and where, in winters long ago, my horse would be compelled by his wilds, hoofing down through the snow for something alive.

We had to leave for the airport a few miles away. My mother and I were mostly quiet as we drove the slick streets where I had once delivered the news. Mother and son spoke dutifully about death and being alright despite it. I imagined she would return home, a new widow seeking some ritual of normality, to put on her apron with no name on it; take out eggs, sugar, flour, and yeast; and make sweet rolls.

By the time the Ozark flight rose, the sleet had blown itself eastward. As we banked out over farmhouses and a crow's murder of cornfields toward Los Angeles, I caught an unexpected glance of the big forest of hardwoods just up the road from our house. Into the void of loss and departure came the singularity of reminiscence.

I would always ride alone into that boyhood timberland, giving the horse a loose rein to pick our way among the oak, walnut, and sugar-maple thickets. Once free of human evidence, I would pull up under the canopy of a favorite oak.

There, with a stolen cigarette, the welfare of a known saddle and all of life's scarce stabilities beneath, I would take in the elemental colors and smells and the small scattered light, and wonder what in the world would be in store.

(A condensed version appears in The Robert Frost Review *[2019].)*

In Varied Depths

Fortune brings in some boats that are not steered.
—Shakespeare's *Cymbeline*

On October 23, 2018, Sandra Day O'Connor, the first woman to serve as a justice of the United States Supreme Court, revealed she had been diagnosed with dementia and was withdrawing from the court and public life. I was moved by this to recall a widespread series of events not previously coalesced in memory.

In July 2006, my wife, Jennifer, and I vacationed for a week at Jenny Lake Lodge, at the foot of the stunning Grand Teton mountains in Wyoming, near Jackson Hole. We joined our old friends Judith and Clifford Miller, who had visited the site annually for decades.

It had become a tradition for them to attend Sunday services at the Episcopal Chapel of the Transfiguration, a log structure constructed in 1925 out on the open plains, some twenty-three miles from the lodge. They invited us along.

On a peerless Wyoming Sunday morning, with scattered clouds matching the snow-covered upper reaches of the Tetons, we entered the little chapel and chose a pew several rows back from the altar. The wall behind the altar was strikingly framed—not by typical religious iconography but by a large picture window that was centered on a captivating view of the Tetons to the west.

We were immediately taken by the harmony—the utter grandeur of the peaks and our rough and humble surroundings of hewn logs, plank floors, and hard seating.

Directly across from us and to our right sat a woman, a man, and a younger woman; they were chatting quietly. They were Justice O'Connor; her husband, John; and their niece.

The deaconess that would conduct the open service emerged, greeted us ecumenically, and asked everyone to introduce themselves. When it was Justice O'Connor's turn, she said the three of them were on a fly-fishing trip. "My niece is teaching me," she claimed. John O'Connor was visibly suffering from his own dementia, which ultimately led to his death from Alzheimer's in November 2009. Justice O'Connor's recently announced retirement from the court was to care for him.

When it was time for communion service, Justice O'Connor went to the railing amid other communicants. As much as propriety demanded otherwise, it was impossible for us not to look at her as she returned to the nearby pew. Her vivid blue eyes were brimming with tears.

The service came to a close with a hymn, and we all began to leave. Justice O'Connor and I came face-to-face in the center aisle. "Why, good morning, Madame Justice. What a pleasure to see you. How are you today?"

"Just fine, thank you very much, and I'm very glad to see you as well." She graciously introduced herself to Jennifer before I could. "Sandra O'Connor. So nice to meet you."

Cliff Miller, always dignified, waited until we were outside, then introduced himself and Judith before thanking Justice O'Connor for her service to the nation, "on behalf of my countrymen."

"Well, thank you very much," she replied, "but I really don't know what all the fuss is about. All I've ever done is to go to work every day and do my best."

With that, the three of them linked arms, John supported in the middle, and walked slowly off.

We regular citizens had encountered this modest sentry of American justice on the flat ground of religious freedom; we would not forget that brief encounter with power, humility, and impending grief in a setting of such perpetual beauty.

Thirty-two years earlier, I'd had the privilege of sitting in the United States Supreme Court to witness oral arguments in Lillian Garland versus Cal Fed, a landmark sexual-discrimination case heard by the nine high-court justices, including Justice O'Connor.

I was the head of communications at Cal Fed, one of the country's largest federal banks. Arguing for us, the defendants, was Theodore Olson of the law firm Gibson, Dunn & Crutcher. I had enjoyed a good dinner the night before with Olson and others. Later on, he became the solicitor general of the United States.

(Olson's wife, Barbara, was killed on September 11, 2001, when her hijacked American Airlines Flight 77 crashed into the Pentagon, killing all aboard.)

Eventually, Cal Fed lost the case. Justice O'Connor voted with the 6–3 majority in favor of the plaintiff—one of her many important sidings on issues of women's rights.

Earlier that year in Los Angeles, prior to the Supreme Court hearings, I had assigned myself to hand-hold Harry Reasoner, the well-known television reporter for *60 Minutes*. The heralded CBS television news magazine sent Reasoner to Los Angeles to do a story on the Garland case.

Reasoner and I met at seven-thirty one morning in the open space between our Wilshire Boulevard headquarters and the parking structure. I knew he was a fellow Iowa native, born in sparsely populated Dakota City, then educated in journalism at Stanford University, where the student body was larger than the total population of Dakota City.

I was also aware that this wonderfully droll news celebrity was a Robert Frost enthusiast. We shook hands and stood there, chatting about Frost, our careers, and "the road not taken." I told him of my great fortune, in 1959, of spending a day with Frost and a small group of other writing students in a World War II Quonset hut on the University of Iowa campus.

Reasoner recalled his favorite lectures on Frost at Stanford. I told him of my fondness for James Hearst, a relatively unrecognized poet from my hometown of Cedar Falls. Hearst had broken his back in a river swimming accident as a youth of nineteen and lived on as a virtual invalid plunging for verse: "[But] the connection with a thing is the only real truth I know," he wrote.

The conversation warmed up. Reasoner said he thought he detected a radio voice and asked if I had had any experience on the air. I replied that in 1961, while I was serving as a Navy journalist, I had worked briefly as a surrogate reporter for his competitor, NBC News, and its radio magazine *Monitor*, then a popular weekend staple of the network. It was hosted by the iconic Dave Garroway, drawing millions of faithful listeners.

"Why surrogate?" he wondered.

I explained that NBC had asked the Navy to allow one of its civilian reporters aboard the USS *George Washington* (SSBN-598) for "an extensive series of interviews" as the nation's first Polaris-missile submarine made a cruise.

The *Washington* was as long as a football field plus a twenty-seven-yard gain and nearly four stories high below the waterline. It was labeled top secret from stem to stern. Each of its eight nuclear surface-to-air missiles was estimated to have more firepower than all bombs dropped in World War II. Its nuclear-powered propulsion system, first developed under the paternal hand of the vaunted admiral Hyman Rickover, had revolutionized submarining.

"Thanks, but no thanks," the Navy brass was about to respond to NBC, citing too many security concerns. But, in a then-uncharacteristic impulse for an Iowa boy who had seen an ocean for his first time only a year earlier, I broached an idea to my commanding officer, Commander Merle McBain, in charge of the Fleet Information Office of the US Navy and NATO Atlantic Fleet headquarters in Norfolk, Virginia, where I was stationed.

I had clearances for US top secret and NATO cosmic top-secret material in a separate connection, had been writing and narrating weekly Navy news reports over the local station WCMS, and narrating monthly military-information broadcasts in English that were translated into NATO-member languages.

"What if," I proposed to Commander McBain, "we write a letter back to NBC to suggest that I do the interviews on behalf of the network?" This was unusual, to say the least, but if the plan worked, NBC would still have its interviews, and the Navy would have coveted prime-time radio exposure. Win-win.

McBain was a mustang officer—that is, one who rose from the enlisted ranks to achieve the gold bars on his shoulders and sleeves. This path to command seemed to have made him more collegial and open-minded to the thinking of the lower-ranking sailors he led. They included me—a young, ex-seminarian college graduate who had washed out of OCS training for a profound lack of the skills needed to master nautical navigation.

"Let's give it a shot," was my superior's reaction. He had a mustache and chain-smoked Camel cigarettes—unfiltered like his opinions. He dictated an inter-office memo outlining the idea to Admiral Elton Grenfell, in command of the submarine fleet. We had our reply from upstairs the next morning—a hand-drawn smiley face on the memo, known by insiders to convey not only approval but enthusiasm. We were green-lighted.

NBC accepted. Six weeks later, lugging my seabag, an Ampex 601 reel-to-reel recorder the size of a small suitcase, a more portable German-made Uher 4000S tape unit, headphones, and an Altec Lansing moving coil dynamic microphone, I boarded the train from Norfolk to New London, Connecticut, where the "Boomer," as the *Washington* and her sister missile subs were called, was berthed.

Once in sight of the heavily guarded pier where the submarine was tied up, I remember a quickening pulse and a warm face. I submitted my credentials and clearance papers to an officer and three armed Marines and was passed through. As the *Washington* came into its full size, I began to have doubts of confidence, like a skier at the crest of his first diamond run.

At the gangway, or on ramp, to the ship, I had expected to find the chief of the watch—normally an enlisted chief petty officer. Instead, it was Commander James Osborne, the captain of it all, looking out at me. Fortunately, he seemed like he was not displeased to see me.

I put my luggage down, came to full attention, and saluted the American flag coloring the fantail, then made a crisp quarter turn to salute Osborne. "Good afternoon, Captain. Request permission to come aboard, sir."

"Permission granted, Hurley," the captain replied, returning the salute.

I stepped from wood to steel and felt the faint vibrations of this war machine, an ungainly-looking bulk of metal and technology, clearly out of its element but strangely swift-looking, like the albacore fish for which its hull design was named.

I could sense her idling there, still moored to the bright land and sky, waiting for her potential out in the vast, perpetual dark.

"Welcome aboard, Hurley," Osborne said. "You have full access to this ship. I expect you to govern your behavior as a Navy man would, but as far as I am concerned, you are a representative of NBC, and every man on this boat knows that."

Twenty-four years old and already a media celebrity—I was pumped.

The bosun's mate was standing by.

"Show Hurley to his quarters," Osborne ordered.

I knew there would be narrow ladders to manage and was relieved that my load might be shared. He took the Uher, the lightest piece, and motioned me forward with a smile.

Given the captain's welcome and even before, on the train, I had imagined my special assignment would merit a spacious berth in the officers' quarters, individual air-conditioning, perhaps a nice reading light, meals in the officers' mess, and maybe even a cold beer or two; these were exceptions to the strict regulations, but then, why not? This was a one-of-a-kind ship and—pardon me, I thought—an equally unique media opportunity.

We went several decks below, passing through the control center, or Con, where each imposing panel of dials and gauges was hidden behind a brown cover with a combination lock. We proceeded to amidships, the *Washington's* lowest center-point. This was Sherwood Forest.

Lined up before my eyes in two equal rows of eight were sixteen massive cylinders, painted in medium green, their full height vanishing into the upper decks like mossy redwoods into overgrowth—Polaris nuclear missiles.

My guide stopped, pointed, and said, "Here we are, Hurley. Stow your gear around you. Chow at 1700 hours. Welcome aboard. Let us know whatever we can do to assist." He left, and I stood there, stupefied. My "quarters" was a canvas military-issue hammock strung between four of the missiles. No reading light.

Before I could settle in, if that's the term for it, another petty officer came bearing welcome gifts: two radiation-detecting dosimeters "to be worn at all times." One was the size and shape of a matchbook, the other like a large-diameter ballpoint pen with a clip. Both had nameplates—already completed to include the Navy serial number matching the dog tags around my neck. *Cousins in purpose*, I thought.

Personnel on a Boomer, officers and enlisted alike, are an elite group. Selected under the strictest and most precise physical and psychological standards, they are the very cream of the Navy crop— able to function with extreme competence in an unalterably closed environment for as long as ninety days and more. Without exception, I found them to be generous, highly cooperative, and warm in both spirit and collegiality. A palpable sense of rank-conscious equanimity prevailed—from captain to cook.

We prepared to get under way. I was invited to the Con, where covers had been removed from the top-secret instruments. The *Washington* threw off her tethers and sailed from the harbor under conventional power out to a certain point of undersea depth and geography. Then, the nuclear engineers below in the reactor room ordered radioactive rods to be inserted in place, igniting a cauldron of gargantuan energy—a staggering, pip-squeak mimicry of the core of the Earth. Later, at sea, I was allowed to peer into it through a small opaque porthole. The sight was transfixing.

Captain Osborne, with two others in the tall conning tower jutting above the hull, ordered everyone below. "Last man down" was confirmed, and the final hatch was sealed. I was tense, my microphone open, waiting for the crisp instructions that now resounded throughout the sub, preceded by three blaring klaxons:

"Dive! Dive! Dive!"

There was a gentle downward thrust, experienced as the reverse of a jet plane rising, and the beginning of an effortlessness of movement—including some breathtakingly steep exercises later—that would mark the next many days.

The *Washington* had now entered her true domain. She had slipped into something more comfortable.

This adventure, which I was describing to Reasoner in Los Angeles, was a testing cruise for the *Washington*, lasting a comparatively short fourteen days and ending in a berth at Cape Canaveral.

I scarcely slept for two nights, interspersed with writing and—lying there supported by four silos full of destruction—the contemplation of extreme fragility. During unguarded moments of sleeplessness, I would confer upon the engulfing seas a frightening undine presence—something akin to a boy awake in his bunk bed while a demon thunderstorm raged over the Iowa plains.

From those luxurious quarters at sea, I prepared and conducted twenty-one interviews throughout the *Washfish*, as she came to be nicknamed. Subjects ranged from missile and torpedo officers to the cooks in the galley to the ultracapable officers and enlisted men who navigated and steered the ship and men responsible for many of its other integral functions.

Sixteen of the interviews were aired by Garroway and his cohosts over a weekend of *Monitor* programming. In Cedar Falls, my large extended family of nearly twenty gathered to listen in the side yard next to our house. My mother, Agnes, that matriarchal genius, had assembled multiple radios to ensure that no single airwave was missed. A couple of electrics on long extension cords and a few transistors with fresh batteries were strategically positioned on our old picnic table.

Garroway interspersed several compliments to the interviews as they were aired throughout the weekend. Listening in Norfolk along with my wife and Navy colleagues, I criticized my work heavily but was inwardly proud.

Fifteen years later, there in Los Angeles with Reasoner, the CBS camera crew had been fidgeting as the introductory chat went on and on. Finally, we went inside to tape the interviews on our views of the Lillian Garland pleadings. From the bank's point of view, we corporate officers were not expecting a valentine from Reasoner and the famously hard-nosed New York producer of *60 Minutes*, Don Hewitt. Hewitt was to corporate America what Scrooge and the Grinch are to Christmas. And I had been admonished by our board of directors not to be too defensive about our side of the case because "the Supreme Court justices watch television too." The resulting broadcasts, coupled with the ensuing decision of Justice O'Connor and her colleagues, fulfilled our misgivings.

Such is the way of many things, though, as I was to discover all along the way. A map is never clear until it's folded out. When I met Sandra Day O'Connor all those years later in an old chapel in Wyoming, I had no thought of loss.

It also turns out that it doesn't hurt to be a little bold sometimes. It turned out fine for a callow kid from Iowa.

to a lustrous wooden dance floor under a mirrored ball. At night, it reflected the colors of red and blue spotlights and dancer's dreams.

Centered on one side of the space was a large, elevated stage, and to the right of it, a commodious bar for serving beer and soft drink "set-ups" to pair with bourbon, whiskey, gin, and vodka brought in by adult patrons in brown paper sacks that were required by Iowa law. Backstage, to the left, there was a storage area for extra tables and chairs.

One early Friday evening, attentive to my responsibilities, I arrived early to set out extra chairs for an anticipated overflow crowd. I went backstage and into the storage area.

There, alone and seated on one of the chairs, a white handkerchief in one hand and lifting a golden trumpet to his lips to form the embouchure of his art, was Louis Armstrong.

Satchmo paused his rehearsal and looked over to me. He smiled those famous ivories of his and lifted his head in a greeting. I gave back the wane smile of a boy unaccustomed to the presence of fame and embarrassed at intruding on it.

Then I excused myself wordlessly and fled from that greatness.

Over time, I was to discover that the only thing that need be feared from being near accomplished people is the fear of becoming accomplished myself.

POETRY

I nearly left my boyhood home for the world of writing without knowing that one of the country's most significant regional poets lived two and a half miles away.

James Hearst, often described as the "Robert Frost of the Midwest," lived his lifetime in Cedar Falls, Iowa. Born in 1900 on the family farm, he grew into the rigors of daily rural life. He had a scholarly mind, graduated early from high school, and began studies at the local college, nourishing his love for literature.

At age nineteen Hearst went to the Cedar River on Memorial Day to swim with his young friends. He dove from a dock into waters made shallow over the winter, breaking his spine in a paralyzing accident he later described as "where footsteps end." His full-hearted farming days were over, but he plowed into verse instead, expressing his love and reverence for the soil and all growing things.

By the time I met him in 1958, Hearst had published *Country Men*, the first of his ten volumes of poetry and two books of prose. His poems were being increasingly welcomed by national and regional magazines and journals.

I was introduced to this kind and gentle poet through our family friend, Edward T. Kelly, a pillar of the community and my employer during high school and college summers. I have never forgotten Ed's many fostering kindnesses and role modeling.

Ed and I arrived at Hearst's home on Seeley Blvd. on a brilliant June afternoon. We parked and walked to his front door, already opened for us.

"Come on in," Hearst called out amiably from the living room. He excused himself "for not getting up." Fifty-eight years old, he was sitting in a brown upholstered easy chair, wearing a wool sweater of mixed colors over heavy khaki trousers. We sat down and were offered lemonade by Hearst's wife, Meryl.

His face, deeply cleaved at the cheeks and baked in the kiln of a thousand suns, had the texture of an autumn corn husk. The knitted sleeves of his sweater ended in hands creased and gnarled, the paralytic fingers turned under for good like the tines of a harrow.

"My friend Ed here tells me you like writing," Hearst said. "Have you had a start?" Ed answered for me, telling Hearst I'd just had my first poem published in my college's quarterly.

"Okay, a good start, then. Which poets do you like?" I stammered, trying to sound educated. I had never read Hearst's poems and knew little about him. I was somewhat familiar with Robert Frost, Carl Sandberg, and a few others, and quoted a bit of Frost, never imagining that I was to meet and talk with Frost himself only a year later.

Ed asked Hearst to read "Truth," Hearst's seventeen-line metaphor for seeking personal insight. We are invited into the poem to join two neighbor farmers; the speaker, who has plowed his land, the listener, who has not.

Hearst began, his voice as rhythmic and certain as a whip-poor-will's: *How the devil do I know/if there are rocks in your field,/plow it and find out.* At the poem's conclusion, Hearst's voice lowered an octave, and its speaker advises: *That means/the glacier emptied his pocket/in your field as well as mine,/but the connection with a thing/is the only truth that I know of,/so plow it.*

Somehow, that moment fired my senses for poetry. I fell silent.

We drank another glass of Meryl's sweet lemonade, heard two more poems, chatted about college and writing, then rose at Ed's signal to thank Hearst and say goodbye.

"Staying at it is the thing about anything," Hearst said as we left.

Sitting there across from that gentle teacher and farmer of words who had known much of hardness yet stored away silos full of bright truth, I began to see what it might mean to follow him in the doing of it.

TELEVISION

It all happened because an elephant was a prolific impressionist painter. Out of that grew an idea realized in 1971 as I lunched at a bar and grill on Gower Avenue, a few steps north of the famed Sunset Strip in Hollywood.

I was vice president of creative services at Vanguard Studios, a photography and film production shop on Cahuenga Boulevard, across the street from the geniuses at the Hanna-Barbera animated cartoon firm. Vanguard was well known on a smaller scale, as a specialist in public relations and publicity support for a wide variety of clients.

Bill Seaton, director of public information for the San Diego Zoo, heard of a series of short biographical film clips I produced on George Murphy, Zubin Mehta, and Shirley Temple Black for an awards program at the Greater Los Angeles Press Club. Seaton imagined that the format might be adaptable to boost attention for the zoo's extensive collection of world quality talent.

We talked and were hired. One of our first successes was a filmed piece on a newborn baby giraffe at the Zoo, for "Pet Set," the daytime television show hosted by the irrepressible comedian, Betty White and her husband, Allen Ludden. This resulted in a half dozen later appearances on the show, eventually with live animals from the zoo.

That day at lunch on Gower, I was mulling other ideas. I had met a very junior trainer at the zoo, a young woman in the male-dominated field who had coaxed an elephant named Carol into swinging a brush in its trunk to produce watercolor images in the Children's Zoo. The woman's name was Joan Embery.

Some officials at the zoo, and some of my colleagues, thought this was cute gimmickry for kids, but lacked staying power. Sitting over my beer and sandwich, I began to think there might be more to it. Why not swing for the full-color canvas of national television? Why not "The Tonight Show with Johnny Carson," and the ultimate in exposure on this American phenomenon?

I returned to the office and phoned Craig Tennis, head talent coordinator of the Carson show. After a week of repeated calls, I received word that he had left a message while I was away and reached him that afternoon. "What's on your mind?" he said, rather curtly. I knew he received hundreds of such calls, and I'd prepared a sixty-second outline of the idea, including examples of animals we'd bring to Burbank for live appearances. I made my pitch.

There was a pause that seemed twice the length to my proposal. Then, Tennis said: "When can you come over?"

Carson loved the concept. In less than two months, working with Tennis, Embery, and Seaton, we had our ducks in a row. Joan Embery would appear with Carson and 500 species of the zoo's menagerie more than 70 times, captivating a nation in the throe of late-night television's heyday, making her a personal appearance celebrity and vaulting the San Diego Zoo into unprecedented fame.

It is well known that Johnny Carson was not personally gregarious. But his genius emerged when the red light went on, never more conspicuously than with his feigned alarm in the company of the zoo's slithering and four-footed visitors. The segment was so instantly popular that one night, when it went overtime, the scheduled appearance of a young comedian was scratched. Her name was Ellen DeGeneres.

Another night, a guest marmoset jumped from Embery's arm to Carson's head and, in zoological terms, "marked its territory" there. (This, along with numerous other episodes, can be found on YouTube.)

The unwritten ethics of the consulting business preclude taking public credit for a client's achievements, while being willing to take the weight of the duds. However, Bill Seaton, the man who hired me, wrote a book about his trove of experiences, including our blowout success on Carson. Bill inscribed a copy to me: "Thanks for making me famous!" he penned.

This story, told for the first time in print, demonstrates that doubt and skepticism should never be allowed to get in the way of an elephant making a good impression.

And that going for the fences sometimes scores a grand slam.

ROYALTY

It's unnerving when a messenger arrives at the office with a heavy, sealed envelope and insists on delivering it only in person. Even in March 1988, it knitted the brow.

A court summons? An attorney's subpoena? The IRS?

No, as it turned out; it was a summons, guilt-free and gilt-edged:

The Master of the Household is commanded by Her Majesty to invite Mr. and Mrs. James F. Hurley to a Dinner to be given by The Duke and Duchess of York on board H. M. Yacht Britannia at Long Beach on Thursday, 3rd March 1988, at 8:15 p.m.

Dress: Black Tie; Long Dress. R. S. V. P. In writing to: The British Consulate-General, Los Angeles.

I knew royalty was in the city to highlight a cultural exchange week, called "U.K.-L.A.," and that the 412-foot *Britannia* had sailed all the way from the United Kingdom to the U.S. Naval harbor in Long Beach. I was an executive at one of the co-sponsoring companies and part of the multicorporate public relations team promoting the event.

Still, I was nonplussed at the envelope; I was a corporate officer but not high up enough to imagine receiving such an honor.

Just as I was signing for the package, a staffer rushed in to say that Bob Dockson, chairman of the board, wanted to see me, pronto. I finished signing and scrambled two floors up the backsteps of the building and into Dockson's commodious office. He was smoking a cigar.

"Come on in, Jim," he said. "I'd like you to represent us at a function Thursday night." He said his wife, Kay, had been taken ill, that the two of them would be unable to attend the Britannia affair. Now I understood the messenger's peremptory arrival.

Of course, I accepted the assignment, and raced back to the office to phone Jennifer, knowing she would have to go shopping and hoping my tux looked decent.

We arrived on time at Long Beach, cleared the close security and boarded *Britannia*, its masts flying the American and British flags. The Royal Band was playing the overture to Monckton's *The Arcadians*. British and United States naval officers, resplendent in full dress uniforms, milled about on the deck with L.A. mayor Tom Bradley; a state senator; Gail Wilson, the wife of the Governor Pete Wilson; the oilman and philanthropist Armand Hammer and other dignitaries. Women colored the black-tie scene with beauty, sophistication, and diplomatic savvy.

When all were assembled aboard, the band played the national anthems of both countries, beginning with the "Stars Bangled Banner." A light breeze from offshore stirred the flags and the people.

We were ushered below decks to the long dining space. *Britannia*, fifty-five-feet wide at the beam, accommodated fifty-six guests that night in a U-shaped arrangement of tables. Two reception lines were formed by courteous junior military officers, with women on one side to be greeted by the evening's hostess, men on the other to be welcomed by the host.

Out came the exuberant "Fergie," Duchess of York, followed closely by Prince Andrew, nicknamed "Randy Andy" since his late teens, and often called "The Playboy Prince" by media. The couple had married two years before and would be divorced in a tiresome scandal eight years later.

As the lines filed along, I was chatting with a U.S. Navy admiral who had served on a submarine as a junior officer, an experience I had had as a surrogate radio reporter. But I was keeping a close protective eye on Jennifer, missing her, and glancing toward Prince Andrew at the head of our line, to see how soon we might eat. By this time, it was close to nine o'clock.

Then I caught on that the prince's eyes were frequently diverted from his guests and down the opposite line, directly at the beautiful Jennifer. He was, in the parlance, checking her out big time. The first two times, I thought I was making a spate out of jealous imagination. But no; royalty or not, the cad was repeatedly ogling my wife. No, *leering*. I boiled.

The band struck up the *pizzicato* of Anderson's *Plink Plank Plump*, while I briefly considered giving Randy my *fortissimo* finale of *Lump for a Chump*.

The rest of the evening was more pacific, to match the sea we floated on. There was more crystal and silver in front of our dining chairs than in the keepsake cabinets of a thousand American homes. Jennifer and I later confessed to each other that we struggled to know just where to cut a cluster of table grapes with sterling scissors; which of numerous glasses or forks to choose for which course of the elaborate menu:

Quenelles de Saumon Balmoral; Filet de Boeuf Wellington; Betteraves Braisees Mange-Tout au Beurre; Pommes Cretan; Salade; and *Bombe Glacee Royale.*

Toasts were made, tributes paid, more music played; the latter ending with selections from Bernstein's charts of *West Side Story.* As we said our goodbyes, I spotted Randy, still stealing looks at Jennifer. None of this had been in the least reciprocated, but I couldn't wait to go ashore.

In the car, I got my bowtie off and cooled my righteousness. Jennifer was totally unimpressed with Randy, and without question, it had been a lucky, lovely evening overall.

The graceful and amiable Kay Dockson regained health, easing us and allowing full gratitude for the grand adventure of a night produced by her vicissitude.

As to the Playboy Prince, we had seen ample evidence—and would see more to come—that sometimes you *can* judge a book by its cover, even if it's hidden under braid, medals, and sash.

COMEDY

It's a truism that breakfast is the most important meal of the day. After all, we're *hungry;* that alone puts it right up there. But when there's better entertainment at breakfast than at the best nightclubs, that puts poached eggs before roast chicken.

For some ten years starting in the early 1970s, I had breakfast nearly every week at Patys, an informal diner on Riverside Drive in Toluca Lake, just northwest of Hollywood, where I worked. My regular companion was Hank Rieger, a great friend and former boss, who was director of press and publicity at nearby NBC Television. We would meet at Patys at 8:30 sharp. Hank often brought Gene Shepard, another old friend and a writer on his staff.

Jonathan Winters, the madly eccentric genius of comic improvisation, lived nearby in Toluca Lake and breakfasted frequently at Patys. He was already iconic, appearing regularly on NBC's "The

Tonight Show with Johnny Carson," on a host of the network's specials, and elsewhere at numerous venues.

We never saw Winters come to Patys bareheaded. Most frequently, he wore the cap of his cherished Cleveland Indians, and often carried a cane or other implement of his art. He would walk eastward the short distance from his home to Patys, where tall glass windows fronted on Riverside Drive.

The moment he reached the first pane of glass, it was as if the curtain of a stage opened, and the antic performance would begin. We would sometimes speculate in advance on which character would be in charge of that wild, rubber-faced man from Dayton, Ohio. Marge, our usual waitress, would join in.

Because he knew Hank from up the street at NBC, Winters would often join us in our booth, giving us memorable gifts of hilarity. He was suddenly a marine in combat or a drill sergeant, a drunken Eskimo or the queen of the Vikings. "Buck Needlehoffer," a Stetson-hatted cattle rancher, might appear out of nowhere, like an extra lost from the lot of a movie Western.

I was always hoping for "Maude Frickert," Winters's inspired portrayal of a seemingly sweet grandmother who would reveal a barbed tongue and eyes casting around for young boyfriends a third her age.

One special morning, Maude was notably demonic. Winters entered her being as he worked on Patys Original Scramble, a concoction of ground beef, onions, spinach, and hash browns, choice of toast. This day, Maude was more boundless and acerbic than we had ever seen her on television.

The booths at Patys were upholstered in red Naugahyde, smooth and slick by manufacture and use. That day, I was seated in the outside position on one side. As Winters and Maude raged on, I convulsed in laughter. Suddenly unable to control myself, I fell out of the booth, landing in an akimbo jumble on the thinly carpeted floor.

"Oh Lordy, honey!" Maude cackled. "Did you break anything, you poor little thing?"

He was like Tchaikovsky's *Nutcracker* engraver, adding a piccolo in place of a flute to the score of a composer's genius. This day, Winters was memorably boundless with Maude.

When briefly out of whatever persona he chose, Winters was a personable, even warm man, who wanted to know where you were from and who was in your family. As we sat many times in that slippery booth with him, we discovered that beneath his comic brilliance was a man with commonplace humanity and approachability.

Johnny Carson called Winters "truly possessed." Carson's predecessor, Jack Paar said, "If Jonathan Winters is ever accused of something, he has the perfect alibi; he was someone else at the time."

SPORTS

I think it was Gate 4, in American's C concourse at O'Hare. I had flown in from Los Angeles in March 2006 for business in Chicago and was now seated for a trip to Fort Lauderdale for a panel at a National Investor Relations seminar.

The plane was boarding from the rear. I was going over some notes and started to hear a rustle of voices. I looked around but could only see passengers stowing their overhead bags. As the aisles gradually cleared, the voices multiplied in shouts and applause, coming like a fan wave to the front cabin.

Then a figure appeared, about six feet tall and agile for his age. I didn't recognize him right away, but many did, to their obvious delight. He came, smiling broadly, to the aisle seat next to mine at the window.

"Hello, friend! Ernie Banks. We're goin' on a ride together!"

Here was the ebullient athlete the *New York Times* would call "the greatest power-hitting shortstop of the twentieth century and an unconquerable optimist."

At seventy-five, Banks radiated energy and confidence, as if he had just left the dugout at Wrigley in the first inning, his lightweight bat moving in a short form of the mighty reciprocation that made every pitcher sweat. Ernie's immortal quote, "Boy, it's a beautiful day. Let's play two," didn't appeal to them.

He put his bag up and sat down to begin a conversation that would last until we entered the terminal at Fort Lauderdale three hours later, where the fan wave came in reverse. I had a crick in my neck for two days. Banks was one of those celebrity figures who didn't seem to know it. He had a gusto for personal contact that couldn't have been made up; it was too irresistible not to be real. "Mr. Cub" didn't quite cover it; "Mr. Sunshine" did.

A career-long Chicago Cub, Banks was the first of his race to make their roster, six years after Jackie Robinson broke the color barrier with the Brooklyn Dodgers. In his nineteen years playing, Banks hit a prodigious 512 homers, 47 in his 1958 season alone. After playing in 2,528 games, with 2,583 hits and 1,636 runs batted in, he retired in 1971 and was elected to the Hall of Fame in 1977 on the first ballot.

As our flight climbed out in the bright Chicago skies toward Florida, we got acquainted. We ordered Cokes and peanuts— "Not as good as ballpark, Jim!"—then deferred on the meal offerings. No hot dogs available.

What emerged most emphatically on our trip, and later, was Ernie's deeply authentic compassion for the poor, especially hungry children. Our wide-ranging topics always returned to that. The second of twelve children in his birthplace of Dallas, Texas, he was eager to hear of my early family life in Iowa, where I was the second of nine kids.

At thirty thousand feet and well into the flight, Ernie asked me what I did for a living in Los Angeles. From the ensuing exchange, we concluded that he had a need, and my consulting firm might be able meet it. By the time we touched down at Fort Lauderdale, we had the outlines of a plan.

I was quick to enlist Hud Englehart, a longtime friend and Chicago-based consulting partner, the finest strategic communications thinker and presenter I have ever known. We brought in our savvy associate Cliff Miller, an encyclopedic baseball aficionado and friend since 1961.

We worked with Ernie for eight months to energize his relationship with the Cubs, his personal appearances and signings, and funding support for his charity to feed poor children, the objective closest to his heart.

As in all but the rare business relationships, ours was inevitably subject to the complications of aging, exploitation, and capital allocation, which saddened Ernie, Hud, and me. Ernie made $680,000 in his playing career—a pittance by contemporary standards—but did not benefit from wise money management.

Ernie Banks suffered a heart attack and died on January 23, 2015, at Chicago's Northwestern Hospital. He was buried, appropriately, at Graceland Cemetery, in the town Carl Sandburg called, "The City of the Big Shoulders."

I hung up from my final call with Ernie and knew I had been permanently affected by another encounter of pure chance, this one with a man of personal magnetism and gregariousness that blended with his fame like milk and honey.

In the end, Ernie Banks' life spoke as much of hope and human proximity as he did when he whipped those molten arms to thwack a fastball and send it streaking with the parabola of a missile into escape orbit and the outfield bleachers, where poor kids rose and cheered.

III

Poems

But tree, I have seen you taken and tossed,
And if you have seen me when I slept,
You have seen me when I was taken and swept
And all but lost.

—Robert Frost, *Tree At My Window*

IMPRESSIONISTS

—for Jennifer

We never know ahead
What God or Zeus proposes
But April gave our grounds
A perfect storm of roses.

My love got the Impression
Of bounty down in oil
Mr. Lincoln, Grace, and Heritage
Were cut but would not spoil.

I know other things that take no soils.
The cornflower dress you wore at first,
The awful Chinese food, the theater,
Your eyes, those blue induction coils.

"No chaperones," we told matchmaking friends.
"You're being cautious, but we're both mature."
Too much partition brings the risk
Of dampening hopes for shared allure.

With foppish yellow shirt and words,
I dug for courage at La Jolla Cove,
Then, shaking, dropped the ring.
You found it; then I had my treasure trove.

With witnesses we didn't know at all,
We wed; the judge forgot his speech.
A spa with flowers in our suite,
A picnic-basket lunch on Carmel Beach.

That time in London when you met
Me in a light spring rain at Charing Cross,
Our frequent rain-head showers at Savoy.
I'm warmed by them in silhouette.

You wouldn't taste piranha stew
At our camp along the Pantanal.
So indelicate and unlike you,
So distasteful, so banal.

But these are only tendrils from our prime,
Clumping, spiraling, halting in their climb;
A painter and a poet locked in time
In selfsame schemes of color rhyme.

Now thirty-seven years have dawned to night.
Come, brush in magenta cameos;
Everything we've seen, some tint of light,
Some chroma-key of thistle and of rose.

Now let's keep loving fiercely on,
Smarting seldom from the random thorn.
We'll keep this floribunda in the sun
Until all your roses are reborn.

If you had never chosen me,
I never would have seen the hue
Of burnt sienna or of phthalo blue.
Renoir said emotion is the cue:
I owe my becoming fully me, to you.

RIVER, IOWA

What is your motivation, Cedar River?
You're often rude in rushing by.
You're shallow to a swimmer's eye;
It makes us doubt that you're a giver.

You broke Hearst's back, your curse
Against a farmer's scarcely idle day.
He answered in a farmer's way
By plowing into verse.

Slivers in our fingers from your namesake tree,
You swell above the levees,
Pilfer roads and cemeteries;
You cannot seem to let us be.

The Meskwaki must have cherished you
For watering their ponies and their soups
At Turkey Forks before the coming of the troops,
When Wolf Skin warned his people and they all withdrew.

Recall the day you sank an old black man
Who made the agitation of a fishing hook.
He only hoped a carp would look
To fill his family's frying pan.

Our wedding bells expanded on your skin,
And you reflected fireworks for children in the park,
Your surface cloning light from dark.
Was that you repenting for your sin?

The moon would crater into purple folds,
Our dashboard radios awash with sounds,
Releasing dreams down out of bounds
Of secrets and the scent of marigolds.

We'd skate your frozen braids
And toast ourselves by fires
Made from worn-out tires,
Playing out our young charades.

That dam in Waterloo was lovely in its forms;
It sluiced for silver in a morning's light.
You made it level to our sight
When you drank too much from thunderstorms.

Such a fickle personality,
So indispensable and brash.
Such attitudes will always clash,
Such kindness and lethality.

But Cedar, you must realize,
You empty into something, too.
Maybe you are like what moves you,
Something big but without size.

ILLUSION

On mornings when I'm not in charge of life,
And cannot lift my mace to stir the fife
And drum corps lazing in a war-torn pen,
The words in fog and camouflage again,
I'll dream about it, just to get the feel.

I'm like a potter lacking clay or wheel;
A formless danseur in a weak ballet.
I cannot get my deficits unwound
From the illusion of control someday.
And still, the pen is stubbornly aground.

Without a thought, I clink my spoon around
The empty coffee cup, and realize
That even rigid structures oscillate;
That I can hear their rhythms in disguise
Once daydreams and an empty page conflate.

A quickening; the burden losing weight.
I mute the solo, switch from ears to eyes,
Lift up the barrel of the pen and sight
Along its bead for targets in disguise;
A stalker seeking language to ignite.

And then the rapid pulse, the throat grown tight.
A freshened huntsman's long-sought trophy dream
Is crouching there in morning's telling light,
In innocence, emerging in that beam;
The ideal word, now cautiously agleam.

Prelude to Campus

—for Mary Agnes

My little sister might have asked me sooner
To push her on the rusty swings that hung
Among our orchard rows, although that June her
Strings of heart, attuned and lightly strung

For ballads any brother would adore,
Could not fully demonstrate her zeal
Until that autumn day, when just before
I hurried through a final home-cooked meal

(Return to college chores was prompting speed),
She came to shyly beg if I would swing
Her to the sun-blessed air. The playwright Bede,
Among my classroom gods, could hardly bring

A man to acquiesce so solemnly;
From then, I knew that love prevails at three.

Edited from The Spokesman *(Winter 1957). Reprinted in* Catholic World *(March 1958) and* Supernaculum *(1958). Gerard Manley Hopkins Award for Poetry, Loras College (1957).*

Offered Hand

I met Robert Frost one day,
Took the offered
Hand, so creased by
Spade and pen and age
Yet still bone-sure,
Not soothed by popularity
Or keeping guard
against the riddles safe
behind that tanned,
uncommon face.

I was a blurry, would-be
Poet. He was plainly one.
I caught an old desire in
Those color-blinded eyes
To puzzle out an ideal rhyme
Containing God and
Science similarly born.

We walked together, then he sat,
And gestured to his left. I sat,
A momentary viceroy
To regency, to gravitas.

He made a joke at the photographer
about impermanence of flashing bulbs
and apertures for calculating light.
We talked of students writing poetry,
The chance for permanence,
The shutter speeds of youth.

He rose, and I, though still
A callow bobbin boy,
Was halfway in his known world.
"You walked a way beside me,"
He said in *A Boy's Will.*
My steps with him enough
To thread a needle of my own.

And then he left, to read
For thousands in a nearby hall.
His hair, as always, whirled and blown.
This celebrated Frost, who most
loved walking in the woods alone.

AGE

To brush receding hairs of memory
Uproot them of capacity for growth,
Then strip the brush of casualty,
Is next best thing to killing both.

I Watched

A sick old farmer doing all he can
Before the acreage of his brain deforms.
While making no adjustment to the plan,
He works, awaits his dual winter storms.

A stricken woman in an ICU
Holds her shell of husband to an ear,
The life signs winking off in pallid blue;
She's cherishing the sounds she cannot hear.

A baby kicking in her bassinet,
A freedom never felt before,
Except in darkness of a mother's womb,
Where kicking, she could just imagine it.

Friesians

I especially love to see them running free,
Loose from armor, harness, battling men.
Tossing, prancing, manes of finery,
They make me think of how we once had been.

Twelfth Step

—*for Terry R.*

At one point or another
I was a ship with no name on the bow
And a few painted out
At the stern.

I was schooner or scow,
Went from epicure to scraps,
Forgotten port to anchor line,
Cormorant to grebe.

No matter what meridians were crossed,
On placid seas or tossed,
No fortune-telling compass told
Of any difference in how I rolled.

In seventy-three, a priest came by my side
In ICU, unbidden and unknown.
Extreme Unction time, I thought,
The only salve for what I'd sown.

"Could there be something wrong with you,
Besides what's on your chart?"

Behind his stole, instead of mortal sin distilled,
There was a layman with a mortal illness stilled.

If, he said, I had what he'd survived,
(This, not what he was ordained to give),
He'd learned a better way to live
With what our genes and fears contrived.

I felt a rupture of the mind;
a tear, a tear, a wish to hear—
the way a poet must perceive
a sudden rhythm to unwind.

For forty-eight long years this day
I've stuck by his approach
to what we'd both been stricken by,
in which we'd known such disarray.

I've heard a thousand voices say the same
In worlds of rooms without a name.
From streets and mansions, they all came.
I've heard ten thousand voices make the claim.

Terry, brother not in blood,
Father, but not quite,
Thank you for that awful, dawning night.
Your trickled hope has come to flood.

That ship now has a single name
Not painted on, but burned,
To make a lifetime's counterclaim:
Returned.

Dear Mr. Thompson

"Across the margent of the world I fled . . ."
—*Francis Thompson,* The Hound of Heaven

I heard the costumed paw-beats of your dog
And fled them terrified, incisors bared,
Through brambles, treasure hunts in sacred fog,
Then was betrayed, insentient and flared.

You spoke of traitorous trueness, thoughts, and deeds.
I learned of these while memorizing script
From Latin seminary-training creeds
Spooled up in coda spindles quickly stripped.

Inside the vaulted chapels hushed and strung
By pews and kneelers promising my vows
Would be like music from a hymn unsung;
I knelt, then ran from treasons I could not espouse.

I fled with rum; you rolled with opium.
We both made outright tries at suicide
When dravest beauty would not ever come
Until we knew: One piper is not pied.

And finally, he chased me down, dear Sir,
Not at prayer, but in a clinic bed
Where all of text and truth were but a blur,
Where all I finally prayed was to be dead.

That darkness has not come again to hide
Me, Sir, or even made its shadow's claim.
I haven't seen it since I verified
That death is not your Hound becoming tame.

Somewhere on the Madison

"Cast it to that softer water, river right," my guide advised,
As if I hadn't always aimed it there.
He didn't know I'd once devised
Immunity from lures tossed anywhere.

A drift-boat fisherman will think freestyle,
Unwound by chantings from the Madison,
Old northbound cousin of the Nile,
With glassy boulder eyes the glacier had outrun.

"There, a sandhill crane in flight."
Its neck projected on the parallels.
It matched the one I'd stretched too tight
That only met with curt farewells.

I put the fly rod down and flamed a Monte Cristo into life.
As if I hadn't burned some other afternoons alight,
Worn down by what I understood as strife
When random anglings never drew a bite.

"You're giving up on fishing for the day?"
I'd seen the cage of ribs an elk had left in wintertide.
As if my bones weren't on display to
Advertise good hunting on the other side.

"No, I'm looking for the secrets in the scene."
I watched the banked Montana willow trees.
"Like tying flies and knots, you mean?"
At twenty-five, he had no want of inner ease.

"More like untying tired ones."
As if the river taught a course on time,
the risibility of sunken suns
Annealing into unexpected rhyme.

Then came the obligation of an eagle
Overhead, as if from reverence for chance.
So much easiness from wings widespread,
The other fisher's hopes could dance.

I raised the casting rod and threw carefree,
Uncertainly, old rhythms coming back
For all there was to newly learn,
As if I freshly knew of fear's hyperbole.

As if I didn't always know
That cadences return.

FARMER HEARST

No Cassandra gave a sign
The day the Cedar broke your spine.
Your reconstruction came along a line
No surgeon's knife could realign.

What you said of fire living on
It's ashes, you began to light upon.
You made a beeline every dawn
Not for the raven, but the swan.

You pulled the stubborn thistles from
The soils and knew the ones to come.
When pricked by pain of back or numb,
You'd write and straighten up to plumb.

I've broken many spines since then,
of books of yours I've loved again.
The Cedar never broke your back or pen.
He just made Cassandra into Zen.

JULIA ROSE

—for my daughter

I couldn't see you clearly through the nursery glass;
my eyes were bandaged in a gauze of tears.
I thanked the nurse who recognized my novice class
and knew the awe was coupled with my fears.

She wanted me to count your fingers, left to right,
as if to bring this *pater genitor* to earth.
And I can count them still, while breath goes tight,
these fifty-six Septembers since your birth.

At your first cry, the resonance of mine,
We both had lain at first breath's cliff.
We'd reached the Kármán line
Of breeching, borderlands, and myth.

No one should have to go there twice.
And still, I had; would go to it again.
I knew your eyes were asking, even then
If someday I would pay the asking price.

What I wasn't capable of saving then,
You began to save that time, and time again,
The way a rooting tendril saves its soil
And spins its arms into a loving coil.

Dear Julia, I hope five thousand days
Still come for me to lavish praise
On you for helping set my life ablaze
That day I saw through tears what love conveys.

CLINT

He came into it as flawed as all of us
To learn from those who came before.
By finding old ideas were treasonous,
He solved a puzzle he could not ignore.

He drew his followers the way a breeze
Brings up a downcast face to find its source.
It billowed up to help us solve dis-ease;
In powerlessness, we found a power force.

He was a lawyer and an ex-Marine
Who told of battles with a liquid hoax
But held no trials or skirmishes to coax
Admissions of our own to intervene.

Whatever verdicts had not gone our way
From judge and jurors in their foul play,
He'd smile in replication of dismay,
Then tell the ones he'd lost from truth's decay.

He rankled no one but himself and turned
No torque on anyone; just wrenched the facts
From truths concealed, then gently earned
Our trust to find our own unstudied artifacts.

We'd feel a gradual lightening in our bones;
He'd helped us pick our pockets clean of stones.

The night he died, his cat was on his chest,
And at the moment of the closing breath,
It looked up high to follow and attest
The heavy-lifting quality of death.

And with his easing transit, we were calm,
Though needing something in the way of balm,
But nothing necessarily divine;
Something unexalted, like his shine.

HOLY SATURDAY

A Lumen Christi chorused through
the dark inside our church,
But I could only hope a flame-haired girl
Would cast an everlasting light.

An altar boy in cassock black
As stain of sin, my surplice starched
And ironed into camouflage,
I looked the part, but only looked for her.

The Paschal Candle carried in my aching hands
My hands was heavier than I had thought,
And dropped, its tongue still flickering, and then went out.
The Easter flame is promised tenderness.
But Christ was still the better light, I guessed.

To a Young Astronomer, Lost

Some night she may come back to you
By some method other than a dream.
Her heart and body can be found
But not by red of laser beam.

You must get better at the searching art,
Where scopes and science cannot reach.
You have to probe inside to cool
The heat that wants to take us all apart.

What was the trajectory of flight,
The meteor of frantic argument,
This fragment from some outer place
That fell to burn like anthracite?

Whichever one of you was parent star,
You have to let the embers start to cool,
But not so long they make a cenotaph
To block off any opening ajar.

Young friend, what's now to do
is factor in her azimuth,
Make sure you set the attitude.
Be sure the compass points at least toward true.

Now, admit your own depravity,
Your multitudes of laxity, of pride,
Each of your misdeeds, from deep inside.
Then overstate their gravity.

Airport Jim

—for Jim C., RIP

As your accounting skills
Began to slip, then sink,
As numbers crunched astray
To dim on margins one by one,
Good clients you would fly away to see
Began to fly away.

You went to airports anyway to drink,
Some form of vague arithmetic
Derived from vain attempts to think
As sober minds find reason to.

United to O'Hare, that never left the gate;
The 3:35 that didn't fly to Kennedy;
American to Dallas and forever late;
A snowstorm kept the plane in Rome, incredibly.

The barkeeps shook their heads and smiled
at night-shift desperation's foster child.
They laughed at such distortion of
Your balance sheet, which fit them like a glove.

We showed you another form of flight,
A way to journey even in the night.
Those once-mistaken forms of travel
Came slowly, surely to unravel.

Your days had added up to years,
With big subtractions from your fears.
You've helped us all to persevere.
Thank you, Jim, for landing with us here.

THAWING

—for Rose

My sister called; her warmth had been restored
In Washington from recent storms in Iowa,
Then chilled again by other kinds of cold.

Foraging her freezer, she had come upon
A cache of homemade sweet rolls sent from
Iowa the year before and stashed away
Like silver dollar coins are saved.

Our mother's baker-hands are hidden since,
The way a rudder and a star conceal
Directions when they disappear,
Yet leave their navigation maps behind.

I had no easy way of thawing out
Her unexpected chill, any more
Than warmings for my own.

But then, we thought together of a loaf
Of stone outside her door, rolled out
By some forgotten glacier's hands,
And placed in easy sight of all who come

And all who leave or have already left,
Some perhaps returning like a winter
Cardinal comes back again to bring
Reminders to a woman's lonely eyes.

Into that browning crust of stone,
Some latter-day convert of Moses
Chiseled in a sole commandment with
The yeasty word that always rises up;
The mellifluent and thawing word:
Laugh.

Pondering

If future, past, and present coexist
Like pulses in the neck and wrist,
Then, therapist and physicist,
What of dreams can be dismissed?

Flight through Hazel Green

—*for Agnes Hurley*

Written at the deathbed of our mother of nine. In context: Bob, engineer;
Jim, poet; Marge, nurse; Mike, humanitarian; Tim, widower; John,
prison warden; Matt, U.S. Marine; Rose, humorist; and Mary, actress.

Last night, I dreamt intently of her hands,
Which shaped us more with urgings than commands.
She told us now of a flight we'd take
on a ship of hazel green
whose underside was glassed to show
all that could be seen.

She saw us safely to our seats,
Then we rose into her dreamy air.
Our first sight was Chicago
And the Field Museum there.
There were paintings of inventors
and an early engineer.
We were puzzled over all of this
until she made it clear.

(She said of Bob)
At the core of the learned mind,
A great equation lies,
Revealing to us to the power of ten
A man's compassion disguised.

In an instant, we flew to Los Angeles
and circled off its shore.
We wondered what was coming now,
What she had in store.

(She said of Jim)
This is the spot where I first set foot
In the broad Pacific sea.
Its waves will encourage, time into time,
The cadences of poetry.

Back to the Middle West we sped—
to the town of Cedar Falls,
where she pointed to a woman's house,
Wisteria in bloom along its walls.

(She said of Marge)
This is a home of loveliness
Where simplicity is key.
From vines to nurse's touch,
It's reminding me of me.

We banked and glided south a ways
into a charming neighborhood.
We asked if she would comment here
But knew she surely would.

(She said of Mike)
The essence of your dad's best traits

Is epitomized right there:
Perseverance, generosity
With a blind instinct to care.

We dipped into the south of Waterloo
and came to an old brick house.
There were colors shining still despite a dying spouse.
Burnt umber, jonquil—last embraces.
The golden hues of children's faces.

(She said of Tim)
Those colors burst from searing pain
To blend in sun, to tolerate the rain.
Because of the light at this family's core,
Each is assured of a rebirth in store.

We dipped away, then saw a mountain range
Rise up, as if to prearrange
A cave shaped like a mouth, where men were hollow-eyed.
A warden stood; he had to stand aside.

(She said of John)
A man whose texture further smooths
With exposure to the grime
Is like a pearl ground smooth, its color rare
Inside the crusted shell of crime.

The airplane banked, gained altitude, and sped
to Vietnam—its jungles stained, the fields all red.
The skies were errant blooms of black;
Steaming curtains rose to meet uprising flak.

(She said of Matt)
The steam is partly the heat thrown off
From gallant men in war

But also the warmth of joy renewed
When one's man's courage comes once more.

The steam cooled to fog, and soon we found
The striking curves of Puget Sound.
A woman sat beside her dog
To browse her humor's fertile catalog.

(She said of Rose)
The ocean breaks that landmass
Like an unrestricted smile.
When a woman pours out laughter,
She contradicts a listener's guile.

We turned back east to Iowa—our final stop,
Where we could see a curtain drop.
All clouds had come apart to show a crisp September day.
A girl was there in costume for a Beckett play.

(She said of Mary)
Her craft is like a flower's soul,
Expanding daily to unroll.
The beauty she portrays
Evokes our family's brighter summer days.

Apollo 11

We raised our eyes
To heedless skies,
Could not see from glare
Of naked sight
The landed flight,
A ladder there.
But in our lighted squares,
We could see how wonder dares.

WAYS

Most bridges won't be marked one-way;
Only one must always be.
But rivers I have crossed in disarray
Were snagged both ways by old debris.

CONTESTS

Our casting hands are tired and tanned
By a thousand wishful throws,
Chasing the rainbow flash
That only a riffle knows.

Where else should we cast
In the summers to come;
What more can we know
Of a river's hum?

A silver form rises,
Then ignores the appeal,
Knowing each of our guises
As he turns on his heel.

Then a strike comes like lightning,
And a deep-throated thunder rolls,
But we're seeking the trout more
Then saving our souls.

We're fugitives, in water and from land,
Contesting something we won't understand
Until the riffles quiet and
The lines are all in hand.

EIGHTIETH

You flew on rivers of the air,
Along, across this coil we share,
So we could flow again and know
Again the insignificance of where

We live in daily space and time,
The insignificance of miles, and how
We often use proximity to gauge
The paltry role and roll of age.

From one to another ocean, you've flown;
From desert, over rocky earthenware.
You came from homes you call your own,
Your homes because they called you there.

Do you remember Iowa summer nights
When fireflies would light a glassy ship?
Back when a hundred miles made a trip?
Those orchard swings that reached new heights?

Should we hop our bikes and pedal back,
Risk a pant leg caught if the chain goes slack?
We used the fear of falling to avoid the worst,
But fell; and rising, have been reimbursed.

Once we ran in orchards glistening with fruits—
Too callow then for lessons from their roots.
With three of us subtracted from the nine,
We recognize the darkness roots assign.

At eighty years, I have no falcon's sight.
But I see all your love so vast and bright,
So vivid, so intensified; airtight.
On rivers of the air, we've flown tonight.

CONSOLE

My sister fought against the sleep
She finally gave her ravaged dog.
Too many canine ills, too much of dialogue
With vets; with promises to keep.

"You must feel as if the middle of
Your bridge is gone," I said. "You can't
Go back or get across." That riddle had
Me lost awhile ago, when I'd had death to grant.

She was in a coil of pain that day;
I'd been in its unrelenting clasp.
Because my sister knew I'd been a stray,
She knew we had our arms to grasp.

TWEETING MR. CEDAR WAXWING

First of all, may I call you Cedar
To help attract you as a reader?
Go ahead. I'm still and wide awake,
Waiting for the dawn in Iowa to break.

I have a nest of queries for your silver-lining eyes to scan.
Feel free to ask the whole museum if you can.

I won't invade your branch-space privacy
the way a crow commits his piracy.
Do not hold back or hesitate.
I have the feeling we'll relate.

When you were high on holly-berry beer and flew,
Did you have black phantoms breaking through?
I did. And juice of juniper worked too.
It's something I found nothing to subdue.

When you collided with a windowpane,
Was it reflecting clouds or beading rain?
Perhaps I'd soared in too much sun.
That's easily overdone.

I had troubles at some altitudes,
Even more at southern latitudes.
You've heard that hoot about young Icarus,
At comic club, where jays would bicker us.

You say you seldom perched on wires.
Was that because of blurred desires?
I found it hard to keep my balance there
Once insulation had gone bare.

I flew in altered states of mind and light.
Those were key impairments to my sight.
I found a home in darkness, like the chimney swift,
Using all the loony updrafts to generate my lift.

A thousand cawing boasts concocted by a score of ghosts
Invented fact from fever dreams to validate my clever schemes.
I too was badly winged, but re-winged now.
I give my ocher head a grateful bow.

We're both from eggs and our respective clones,
Chirping in the grace notes of our tones.
Mine is not the sole solution to this quiz.
Such things are not the province of a would-be whiz.

We've each had stumpers of our own;
Discovered truth from circle routes we've flown.
I've found that shaky limbs are easier to light upon;
Fragility deployed as aileron.

And all those mockingbirds that used to taunt our memories
Are stricken mute in antecedent treasuries.
I'm just a fellow passerine

In a chorus where we've been taught.
We'll soon be winging from this scene,
But leaving resonances caught.

My thanks for sharing how you feel
About a killing myth;
How we found a balance wheel
And pecked down through the regolith.

A Sonnet for Vishal Khullar, M.D.

You held a brother's broken heart in hand,
But not the way a lover has her sway.
Your steadfast hands held life another way,
To cut out wounds no lover can convey.

Tagore tells us there is no gap between
A heart's desire and the place it's aimed.
"Not distant," he insists, and no ravine,
Even when desire can't be claimed.

But you have found the lines no poet could
Construct and coaxed old cadences to flow
Through unblocked river braids of likelihood
The way a flood clears out a river's bow.

And with your fluent gestures, made a heart
Boom once again inside a brother's chest
Like clustered thunder, heeding no arrest
Once lightning made its dormant flux restart.

You gave this unbound throb, this rise and fall
Of many days' pulsations for us all.

Two Slow Murders

The neighbor's dog was killed last week.
A gray coyote snuck and slammed,
An act for which it's closely diagrammed.
We heard both dog and old man shriek.

Neither one had asked for much that night
Except their path beside a narrowed stream;
perhaps another chapter of a dream
Of young pursuance swept aside by light.

Today, as if the dog had merely strayed,
He said, "I wonder where the hell she went?
To where I'd never give that dog consent?
I wonder why she would've disobeyed?"

I saw him in two kinds of dusk tonight,
The same old purple cardigan and stains,
Carrying the empty leash despite,
Clutching at the known refrains.

Searching, withered, left and right,
As if the perfect tension still remains.

An Old Friend Dies

I am a hoarder of life,
a rejecter of strife.
When a friend-treasure dies,
denials of fact will arise.

The flaw is the thought
that some truth should be sought
from what should have been aired
instead of contentment in what has been shared.

I am the hardest on truth,
an absentminded sleuth.
What is a mourner doing
so stuck in the gluing?

A foot soldier of sorrow
can desert it tomorrow.
All that it takes
is to abandon mistakes.

No oak can be withered.
What friend should be dithered?
No sun runs west to be dimmer;
Name me a moon that will not shimmer.

Echoes heard from keepsake years
make antidote to fears.
They are the riches,
guardrails from the ditches.

No shadow should taunt them.
Whose grief should still haunt them?

PLAY BALL

—for Cliff Miller

My gallant friend of more than sixty years,
Your eyes are dying for a Yankee game,
But not for lack of fastball brain and cheers,
And reams of stats you easily reclaim.

Stealing bases thrills, but stolen sight
Without an umpire near is like a putout
Blown in nine to lose the game outright
And cost a pennant through a moment's doubt.

At ninety-two, you've had more innings-plus
Than I at eighty-four. But we'll still kick
A little dirt before it's kicked on us;
Pick up our idle bats and take a lick.

Let's coax more light from this quartet of eyes,
And when we have to, see the plays with ears.
Today, we should ignore what night implies
And flip the dimmer off to spite our tears.

Let's sit and deal another hand of gin
Before we turn the Yankees on again
To see the way a baseball spins its seams
And go to bat against our hurtling dreams.

OKEANOS

Okeanos, father of the river gods,
Float me back to coal-black sods
So rich that if a farmer's wagon spills some seed,
he'll have a random crop accede.

Float me back to inner dreams,
On patched-up inner tubes and schemes
So promising, they take me all the way
Along a Cedar River summer day.

Start enough upriver of the dam,
But not so far for need of telegram:
"He nearly passed the point of safe return,"
The point no errant river can discern.

Take me back to where I started from.
Guide me back; this time I might succumb.

Dear Reader: P.S.

With just the act of opening this book,
You've paid me a lavish compliment.
A lesser friend might choose to overlook
This gathering as less than heaven-sent.

But I can't let you go this way just yet,
To sift some other hardbound stream for gold.
We need a bit more time in our duet
To promise we'll have other streams unfold.

So go down to the river by your town;
If you don't have one, come to mine.
We'll sit and watch a sunset slumber down,
And see how light and water realign.

And once we're ghostly quiet, we will hear
The river's murmurings, its churn and bend.
Can't you hear them now, so full and near,
How the vocals rise, then fall, then blend,

To teach us indistinctly, faithful friend,
Just where the riffle of this poem will end?

Acknowledgments

Even a chip of a book engenders deep gratitude.

To Stephanie Moles, indefatigable compositor, for perseverance.

To artist Esther Engelman, for her evocative cover painting.

To the author and playwright Seamus O'Connor, for friendship and impetus.

To Ed Harshfield, stalwart friend and chairman, for freedom from a suit.

To Robert Bernard Hass, distinguished author, poet, and critic, for devoted friendship, inspiration, and painstaking guidance.

To the poet Raymond Roseliep, my first writing mentor, an endless debt of gratitude.

And to other rhythmic exemplars: Robert Frost, James Hearst, John Logan, Paul Engle, and Felix Stefanile.

To the irreplaceable Maurice Zolotow, Clint Hodges, and Perry Cross, the kindling and sparks of a way of life. And to each of those who have trusted me to replicate the path.

To my five brothers, three sisters, and their spouses—here and gone—and to our late parents, Agnes and Jim, for ceaseless love and bedrock encouragement. Among them, Rose, first reader.

To Julia Rose, beloved and courageous daughter and mother.

Finally and forever, to Jennifer. There is nothing like her on Earth.

A Note on the Typeface

This book has been set in Electra, a typeface created in 1935 by W. A. Dwiggins, a Boston artist.

It was selected to honor the poet Raymond F. Roseliep—whose first book, *The Linen Bands* (1963), was printed in Electra.